PRAISE FOR
KEENING COUNTRY

"These stories offer the reader a guided tour of the secret sins and obsessions lurking behind the doors of contemporary Ireland. Visceral, compelling, *Keening Country* packs a considerable punch. Read it."
— **John Langan**
Author of *Children of the Fang and Other Genealogies*

"Toe-curlingly nasty, be sure not to eat before reading!"
— **Gemma Amor**
Bram Stoker Award nominated author of *Dear Laura*

"Creepy, brimming with shudders, harrowing, and unforgettable, O'Connor is the master of skin-crawling horror whose characters continue to haunt your sleep long after you've turned the final page. Definitely not for the swoon-brigade!"
— **Nuzo Onoh**
Author of *The Sleepless*

"At times shocking, though unique, with shades of David Cronenberg thrown into the mix for good measure."
— **Phantasmagoria Magazine**

KEENING COUNTRY

BOOKS BY
SEÁN O'CONNOR

The Mongrel

Weeping Season

The Blackening

Keening Country

Revelations
Horror Writers for Climate Action

The Swarm

KEENING COUNTRY

SEÁN O'CONNOR

CADAVER
HOUSE

Cadaver House
Dublin, Ireland

Legal Deposit and Library Cataloguing in Publication Data.
A catalogue record for this book is available from The National Library of Ireland.

Typeset in 11pt Bookman Old Style
Interior Design by Kenneth W. Cain

ISBN: 978-1-7384567-6-5

For Alex

"Come fanatics, come to the sabbath."
— Electric Wizard, "Witchcult Today"

INTRODUCTION

Here Be Monsters!

Ignorance really can be bliss, because for a lucky few, it limits a person's view to the world around them. At least, that is my perspective and how the book you are holding in your hands came into existence. Let me briefly take you back a few years, to a time before I decided to try and become a writer...

I grew up in Rathfarnham, which would be considered a rather affluent area of South Dublin. Well, to be more specific, I'm from Whitechurch, which is a council estate in the middle of said area. Admittedly, it is an estate with a bit of a notorious reputation, a place I believe, given the chance, the surrounding affluent population would love to extract, like a cancerous lump, from the map. And while class divide is rife (that is probably a discussion for another day.... or book?), the one thing I've found both the working and upper classes of South Dublin have in common is an ignorance and disregard for the North side of County Dublin.

I'm not sure where this divide came from exactly. Perhaps it's a result of the massive cultural body of local literature in the form of Roddy Doyle's Barrytown Trilogy? Or perhaps it was how local news was reported, instilling a serious case of *Us versus Them* across the city, with the river Liffey acting as a border? Who knows for sure? What I do know is, for the first thirty years of my life I let this ignorance towards the North blind me. I considered everything beyond the Liffey as a *no-go* area. And if I journeyed beyond Dublin Airport, I'd be going beyond the wall and fall off the edge of the map... *Here Be Monsters!*

It wasn't until I met my wife, that my eyes slowly opened and began taking in the dark and mysterious lands to the North of Dublin. She is from Swords, the main town in a county within a county called Fingal, and is a bit of a homing pigeon. So, without boring you with all the details, I ended up taking the plunge and packed up my shit and moved beyond the airport, where we put down some roots in the heart of Fingallian country.

What does this have to do with a Collection of horror stories? Well, roll forward a few years... something clicked with me living out here. My creativity flourished and some of my work has been published. I feel I owe it to the land as it has provided and inspired me. And if you've read my debut novella, The Mongrel, you will know that areas of Fingal feature in it... and the same can be said for the Collection you currently hold in your hand. These novelettes are too big to be considered short stories, therefore making them un-submittable for anthologies or magazines and too small to make it as standalone books. I suppose they are my homage to Fingal County. So, here they are collected for you and all four will take you around these parts...

Are you still with me, Reader? Good. Let me know show you a place where anything can happen and strange tales of the unexpected can unfold. A dark and mysterious place where bad things can happen to good people and on any given night, the wind wails like a banshee across this ancient land. Are you willing to venture a little further? If so, you've been warned. Proceed with caution and if you've made it this far, I'm afraid there is no turning back... ...you are part of *it* now... ...welcome to Keening Country.

AERIALS

Abigail Steward adored her quiet life and removing herself from the hustle and bustle in Dublin was easily the best decision she'd ever made. She would wake most mornings around ten. And could never understand how most people who deemed themselves successful awakened at the crack of dawn to the sound of an alarm clock, leapt out of bed, dressed themselves in clothes that they would not wear on the weekend, then went to fight rush hour traffic, just so they could spend a third of their day making money for somebody else. And the final kicker was that these people had to be grateful for it. No, that life wasn't for Abi and her husband, Shane, anymore.

Newly engaged, they bought a small two-bedroom cottage in the midlands of rural Ireland. Off the grid and away from what they called *Stress City*.

Their home was ten minutes away from a small village, which allowed them to enjoy their shared hatred of technology – which was somewhat contradictory as they both worked from home and required internet access and laptops. Shane self-published sci-fi novels, while Abi blogged about healthy living and life off the grid. Their income was decent, but by no means lucrative. Abi was happy with her lot. Nothing bothered her while living out in the sticks, but on a cold October morning she woke to find Shane missing from their bed. Someone was shouting outside, and she could hear someone speaking quietly in return, trying to calm them down.

Abi leapt out of bed and eased her feet into a pair of slippers, then rushed to investigate the commotion while pulling a silk dressing gown on over her nightdress.

Shane was standing at the end of the driveway, arguing with two men wearing hardhats and hi-vis jackets. One was chubby, with a large round face and the other was no more than sixteen with a face full of pimples that were noticeable a few yards away. The three of them were pointing along the old country road that ran in front of the cottage.

Shane's agitation was plain to see.

Abi tiptoed her way down the cold path towards the front gate while tying her gown tighter to shield from the sharp breeze, careful not to step on sharp and pointed stones. "What's going on, babe?" she called, approaching the wooden gate.

Shane didn't answer and immediately took her arm, ushering her out from beyond the gate and into the conversation. "Now, go on lads, tell my wife what you just told me. Tell her what you're doing here today," he snapped.

With a loud sigh, the chubby man began, "I'm sorry to start your day like this, miss. Your husband is upset with us and won't listen to reason."

"And why is that?" Abi asked.

"We are installing a new aerial on this road today."

"We didn't order anything from our provider. Who are you guys with?"

The man continued, explaining that their company was installing aerials all over the country as part of a national network infrastructure upgrade.

Abi understood the reasoning but felt obliged to side with her husband's objection to an ugly metal pole being planted in front of their home. The cottage was positioned perfectly in a picturesque part of the land. In every direction, lush green fields and trees populated the landscape. The smell of permanent freshness, even in October, was invaluable to the Stewards. With that in mind, she fully endorsed Shane's anger over a man-made eyesore ruining the scene.

"I'm sorry, my husband and I just don't want something that will have such an impact on the landscape. Have you got a contact number for your manager? We'd like to speak to him so that maybe we can dispute this?" she asked, her tone resembling a professional customer service agent.

The chubby man looked her up and down, took a step back, and signalled to his colleague by the van, which was parked up a few feet away up the road. "Certainly, madam," he eventually replied, before diverting his attention to his phone.

Abi turned, kissed Shane on the cheek and gave him a reassuring rub on his back. "You go back in, love, it's okay."

He acknowledged the sentiment, reciprocated, and made his way back to the cottage. She smiled as she watched him wander off. She knew he was upset, but found his passion endearing at the same time.

"My name is Andrew." said the chubby man, his voice laced with a smoker's husk. He handed her a business card. "Here are my company details. Give reception a call and ask for Jim Holden. He's the project manager and will be able to explain the infrastructure upgrade for this area in detail."

Abi took the card, its logo catching her attention straight away – large red block text revealed an organisation she knew well. "You guys are from Ziegler?"

"Sure are. I take it you've heard of us before, then?"

Abi smirked and placed the card into the front pocket of her dressing gown. "I have, yes. And thanks, I know exactly who to call about this, Andrew. You guys have yourselves a good day. We'll be in touch."

The chubby man didn't respond. Instead, he pulled a pack of smokes from his pocket, lit one up and watched a determined Abi make her way back up the garden path.

From the front window of the cottage, Abi and Shane stood watching both engineers plan the aerial installation. In silence, they sipped their coffee – the presence of the business card could not be ignored. And Abi knew what Shane was going to say before he opened his mouth.

"Abi, are you—"

"Yes, babe. I'll give her a call straight away."

Abi went to find her mobile, which was usually kept in her bedside locker and was the only phone in the house. She rarely had it powered on, maybe once or twice a week for a quick chat with her little sister, Melissa – who had recently become Mrs. Power and had become increasingly harder to get in touch with since she'd tied the knot. She figured her sister's radio silence came with the territory of a young person chasing career goals while living it up in the city, especially working for a global organisation like Ziegler – a company known for their lavish corporate and social events.

Debating on whether she should call Melissa on her personal number or at the office, she considered, just for the fun of it, calling the office's helpdesk to lodge an official complaint. But in the end she didn't follow through on the idea.

Melissa's personal number was unreachable, leaving the Stewards sitting and worrying about the construction in front of their home. Abi kept trying for the rest of the day, because if she didn't, she could be sure, Shane would be in her ear.

Later that night, the call finally connected. At first, Abi was relieved at the sound of her sister's voice, but it was not the usual chirpy greeting that she was accustomed to. Melissa was almost incoherent, rambling and, out of all the frantic mumbles, Abi could only make out the words, *"Please stop. We have to stop."*

"Melissa? Please, it's Abi. Talk to me?" she begged into the phone – her pleas unheard. And the worrying call continued with strange noises and muffled cries, leaving Abi imploring her sister to make some sense, then silence.

Abi began to panic. It was completely out of character for Melissa. Even when she was out partying in town, she could still manage to hold a semi-intelligent conversation with her big sis. Abi would listen to her ramble on about the guys at work and how Melissa's husband, Edward, would be jealous of them.

Edward Power – a well-groomed, confident man who never seemed to wear anything other than an expensive flashy suit.

It had been a while since Abi last spoke to Edward... and for good reason. On her sister's wedding night, she saw enough of Edward to know that he was not the kind of man you would want to get close with. His interpretation and interactions with other women usually ended with him wanting something more from them. Despite this, he seemed to make Melissa happy, and that was enough for Abi to keep her mouth shut.

She had never heard Melissa talk like this before and needed to know if she was okay. Feeling like she'd reached the last resort, she scrolled down through her phone contacts, stopping and tapping one saved as *Prick!*

The call rang out, sending Abi into a state of panic. Frantically, she paced around wishing her sister was okay. She tried calling both numbers again, but only received voicemail greetings. A million thoughts swarmed: *Is my sister okay? Is Edward with her? Was she yelling at* him *to stop?* It was all too much, forcing her to spend the night crying in Shane's arms.

The next morning, Shane woke to sunlight creeping through a gap in the curtains. Rolling over, he reached for Abi, only to find her missing from the bed. He shot up, scanned the room. Empty. From elsewhere in the house, he could hear her rummaging around and went to investigate – finding her in the kitchen with a bag packed.

"What's going on, darling?" he asked, wiping sleep from his eyes.

"I have to go," she replied, her voice quivering.

"Wait, what? What time is it?"

"Early. I have to beat the traffic."

"Where are you going?"

"I have to go. I need to see if she is okay…"

"Do you want me to come with you?"

"No thanks, babe. I'm sure my sister is just being a drunken fool again, but I need to go check on her and see if she is okay. I know she can be a messy drunk sometimes."

She gazed towards the window, followed by a long sigh. "Last night was scary. I've never heard her talk like that before. And now I can't get through to her phone."

Shane gave an understanding nod of approval. He knew Abi and her little sister were close. And she would always take on the *Big Sis* role as soon as things appeared out of place.

"I'll be back in no time, babe. You just make sure them Ziegler wankers don't go putting up that ugly thing up. That's your job, okay?"

"Ha, fair enough. I'll call down to the council office when they open and see what I can do," Shane said in agreement.

They hugged and went to her car.

Abi's old Fiat Punto spluttered into life, the exhaust barked, spluttering fumes.

Shane gave her a concerned look, to which she replied, laughing, "It's grand, don't be worrying, hon." She then reached outside the window, pulled him towards her and gave him a kiss. "I have the phone with me. I'll call you later to let you know what is happening. I'm sure I am just over-reacting and everything is okay, but I have to go check on her."

"Be careful on the roads, okay? Try not to drive like a lunatic," he said, watching her back out of the driveway onto the road. Moments later she was over the hill and out of sight.

As she drove along the coast, Abi found herself wondering whether her parents' house still looked the same. It sat on the coastline overlooking the sea near Portrane. She hadn't been back to see it since her parents had passed away a few years ago – Melissa was adamant in staying put, which suited Abi just fine

Melissa and Edward had bought Abi out, allowing Abi the freedom to set-up wherever she wanted. Despite this, as she drove closer to the old family home nostalgic memories came flooding back. She recalled good summers, playing on the beach that they pretty much had to themselves. Her favourite memory was the view from her old bedroom window of a storm incoming from the sea. Together, the sisters would curl up and watch lightning and listen to the thunder roll. No matter how fierce the weather got, they always felt safe and secure together.

The coast road meandered as Abi's Punto motored along, the sky blocked out by heavy clouds, which threatened rain at any moment. Cool air blew in from the sea and as Abi turned the last corner to her destination the difference to the house grabbed her attention. When she last saw it, the exterior had been painted white, the grass out front, lush and green – but at some point, Melissa and Edward had changed all of that. Now it was a dull navy colour and the garden was unkempt and overgrown. The neglect was so evident that it barely resembled in the house in Abi's memory. The sight chilled her. She knew Melissa wasn't one for cleaning, but the very least she expected of their old family home would be for it to remain somewhat presentable. And she was willing to wager that Edward was still as clean-cut as ever.

The front gate stood ajar, rocking in the breeze. Its loud squeak called desperately for someone to oil the hinges.

Abi rolled onto the gravel driveway, disgusted and embarrassed at the extent of dilapidation. "For fuck's sake, Melissa. The place is a state," she muttered.

At first, she knocked gently, but when she got no reply, her knocks turned into frustrated closed fist thumps. "Melissa... Melissa!"

After a while, she gave up and resigned herself to the fact that there was nobody home, then rummaged around in her pocket for her phone and attempted to call. It was useless.

The breeze felt slightly colder now and the sound of the sea was interrupted by engines coming up the road. She thought to herself, *what now?*

The vehicles turned sharply, speeding up the driveway and she saw they were police cars. Within seconds, numerous men jumped out, forming a perimeter around the house. She stood in shock at the frenzy of movement, struggling to decipher what was going on as they sealed off the house.

A tall man ran to Abi, shouting at her to move away from the porch. She froze on the spot as he came closer. Despite the confusion, she noticed that he wore plain clothes and assumed he was an inspector.

"Miss, are you Melissa Power?" he demanded.

"No... No. I'm her sister."

"Are you the one who called us?" his gaze shifted from her towards the house.

"No. I just got here? What is going on?"

The inspector pulled a firearm from a holster that hung from his belt. "He's still inside," he shouted to his men, all of whom snapped into action and readied themselves to engage. "Miss, I'm going to have to ask you to go down the path and wait outside the gate. We have a serious situation here."

"But—"

"This is not a request. Go. Now!" he roared, his body language shifting to an almost primal state, telling her everything she needed to know – he was ready for combat.

"Miss, I said, GO!" he bellowed, prompting Abi into action.

Abi ran down to the end of the path, grabbing hold of the squeaky gate and hiding behind it. Watching the events unfold, the policemen kicked in the door, entering the house with their guns drawn. Inside, she could hear shouting and screaming, but no gunfire – thankfully. She realised her hands were clasped together and she was praying, begging for her sister's safety.

The standoff felt like an eternity. The commotion inside fell silent, the remaining policemen outside, armed and ready.

When figures emerged, Abi could make out the inspector easily, his silhouette cut an intimidating presence. There was another figure beside him: slender, timid and resisting arrest. And as they came into view, the inspector signalled to his men that they'd *got him.*

Abi recognised the unmistakable face of Edward Power.

What has the prick done?

Abi started up the driveway slowly. She could see Edward being dragged out in cuffs, covered in blood. The surrealism caused her head to spin. Where was Melissa? What did he do? She wanted to call to him, but the words stuck in her throat.

Edward was shouting at all the policemen, "I didn't do anything. I swear, I didn't do anything." But they ignored him as they opened the back of a van and placed him inside. While his ankles were being secured to the floor, Abi stood looking in at him.

"Abi? Abigail! What are you doing here? I didn't do anything. Tell these men I didn't do anything."

The words once again stuck in her throat. By the time she cleared the rawness, the door had slammed shut. She'd never seen Edward in such a state of panic.

The inspector stepped between her and the van. "I thought I told you to wait outside the gate?"

"That's my brother-in-law. What has he done? Where is my sister? Where is Melissa?" Abi cried, finally able to blurt some words out, but as soon as she said her sister's name, she started to shake with panic. "Please. What is happening?"

"Please, miss. Try to relax. We still have a situation here," he replied with a calmer voice.

"Please, tell me, what is happening?"

"Mr. Power is under arrest for—" He stopped abruptly and placed a hand on Abi's shoulder, ushering her to step aside. From behind, an ambulance made its way up the driveway.

"For what?" Abi cried.

The inspector switched his attention to the paramedics, moving quickly as he informed them where to go as they entered the house.

Abi tried to follow, but was stopped by one of the armed policemen. Shortly afterward, her fears came to pass as the paramedics emerged, wheeling out a stretcher. A body lay covered in a blanket. Without looking, she already knew.

"Melissa! No. Melissa, please talk to me," Abi cried.

The inspector grabbed hold of her, forcing her into a hug. He whispered into her ear to shush, but it was no use – Abi was hysterical.

She watched the body being loaded into the ambulance, her head spinning. Her knees wobbled, then gave way and vomit dashed the driveway.

Abi called her sister's name over and over, to no avail. When her face hit the ground, sky and sea began to blur and she passed out.

Abi hadn't fainted since she was a child. It felt strange to be plunged right back into her childhood in one afternoon. And as much as she wanted to focus on the fond memories of those dog days, the crushing and brutal reality was always a couple of seconds from flooring her. She could not help but think that she was being trampled on by the gods above. She wanted to live a quiet life, off the grid, but now was overwhelmed with guilt for doing so. How could she have left her little sister alone with this man? If only she had stayed, then an eye could have been kept on Melissa and none of this would ever have happened. They could be walking along the beach now, creating and sharing fond memories. But that time had now passed, leaving Abi to combat the ever-changing wall of emotional grief, hurt, and anger.

The inspector advised her to book in somewhere and rest up as it could take a few days to process everything. Abi didn't argue, she badly needed rest. She wanted to follow the ambulance to what she assumed would be the morgue, but was advised that it could be hours before they'd let anyone in to identify her sister.

Instead, she drove aimlessly around Portrane, her concentration dipping in and out, looking for a place to park up for the night. But every time she thought about her sister, the car pulled over and a rancid pile of bile was left on the side of the road.

How did this happen? My sweet little sister. How could I let this happen to you?

She ran her forearm over her face, lifting her long blonde hair up, flicking it back behind her head. The sky opened up above, and she quickly found herself in the grip of a miserable, wet cold night; a sure sign that winter was on the way. It was time to get some focus and regroup.

At the edge of town, a bed and breakfast would provide her with what she needed – a warm meal, hot shower and somewhere to lay down for a while. Once she'd recouped, she promised to go get answers out of Edward.

The fucker has to answer for this.

The roads surrounding Portrane were poorly lit, making it hard for her to see more than a few feet ahead in the dark, but she couldn't help noticing large antennae that lined the streets – every few miles, one stood tall. Camouflaged as trees, they blended in with the landscape. Near the top of each mast, a red light blinked, signalling operation. She thought, *this must what them guys from Ziegler were trying to put outside my house*, and supposed they didn't look like the monstrosity Shane had initially feared. Still, they seemed to be everywhere around the city and suburbs.

Shane – she hadn't emailed him – *he must be worried sick.* She didn't have time to dwell on it now, the weather was getting worse. Shelter was her top priority and she'd call him with the bad news once she was inside.

At the edge of town, the B&B she remembered from her childhood was no longer in operation. The old house stood boarded up, struggling to repel the winter rain. Thankfully there was a new hotel a little further up the road and that would have to do. When she arrived in reception, she looked a mess: hair windswept, make-up running, emotionally bankrupt. After booking in, she found her room and fell asleep as soon as she hit the pillow.

Abi woke to the sound of vacuuming outside her door. *Christ, housekeeping starts early in this place.* She checked the time and saw she had slept late. After a ten-minute ordeal getting the phone connected to the Wi-Fi, she finally emailed Shane, informing him of everything that had happened. *I wish we had more than one goddam phone between us.* She supposed this was the downside of life off the grid, then skipped breakfast in favour of a long walk in an effort to clear her head.

Everything from her childhood in Portrane was familiar, but yet, in a strange way, very different. And that's when she noticed it...

It wasn't the town that was different, it was the people; most of whom avoided her. *Why wouldn't anybody look her in the eye?* Even the receptionist in the hotel barely spoke more than two words to her.

She took the long way back to Melissa's house on purpose, just so that she could see some familiar faces in the shops and post office. Even then, when she said hello, there was no response.

The post office was run by a man called Arthur, who she'd known since childhood. She walked up to the counter and said hello, but got a grunt in reply. He didn't recognize her, nor did he care when she tried to jolt his memory. She couldn't help but think the man was present in body, but completely void in mind.

Abi left the office and walked to the house to fetch her car. What was going on here? Had she been off the grid for so long that she was now the strange one? The engine fired up first time. She checked her phone – no activity. It was time to go get some answers.

Driving slowly and scanning the area en route to the station, Abi noticed that everyone was behaving oddly. Pedestrians walked slowly, with a vacant look in their eyes, almost as if they were high, or zombified. It was all too much for her to process. She figured it must have been all in her head, with grief for her little sister playing the major role. She pulled up outside of the police station, wondering how she could get to see Edward. She was determined to get answers from him. All she knew was that her sister was dead; he'd denied doing it, but he was the one currently detained.

In reception, she was greeted by a large man wearing thick framed glasses. "Can I help you?" he asked, clearly short of breath.

"I would like to speak to the inspector who arrested Edward Power yesterday," she said.

The man allowed his glasses to slide down his nose so that he could look over the top of them. "And you are?"

"My name is Abigail Steward. I'm Melissa Power's sister."

The man didn't reply; instead, he picked up the phone, punched in a few digits and told whoever it was on the other end that the sister of the victim was here.

While waiting in the lobby, Abi grew impatient and was about to let rip at the man, when a door behind where he sat flew open and the inspector walked in.

"Ms. Steward, nice to see you. What can I do for you today?"

"I never caught your name yesterday at my sister's house."

"I'm sorry about that, it was a tense scene, I had no time for formalities. How are you holding up?" he asked, his concern seemingly genuine.

She hadn't noticed it yesterday, but she realised now he looked very young to be an inspector. And he was very handsome in a rugged sort of way.

"I understand, Inspector...?"

"Deegan. Daniel Deegan," he answered before offering his hand, which Abi shook as firmly as she could. "What brings you here today, Ms. Steward?"

"Abi, please. Call me Abi. I need to speak with Edward Power."

Deegan eyeballed her. "I'm afraid that is out of the question."

"Please," she begged. "He was screaming that he didn't do anything."

"And you believe him?"

"I'm not sure what to believe. But I do think he'll talk to me," Abi claimed.

"I doubt that, he's not talking to anybody. He's been silent since arriving at the station and we're waiting for his solicitor to arrive."

Abi refused to take no for an answer and continued to beg the inspector for five minutes alone with her sister's husband. Eventually, he agreed to a supervised ten-minute meeting, but he made Abi promise to only talk about what happened in the house. She agreed and was promptly escorted into a meeting room.

The walls were dull and grey with a dank smell in the air. A table with a few black chairs around it stood in the middle of the room. She sat down and waited while the guards fetched their suspect.

As soon as she was left alone in the room, she started to get nervous. What if he did murder her sister? Would she be able to detect the truth?

The door opened, Edward shuffled in and sat across from her. He had a fearful glint in his eyes and a quiver in his voice when he said hello. Not the usual confident and dapper man she once knew. She pitied him. When Deegan sat next to him, she listened as he explained that the interview had a time limit and that now was the time to be honest, otherwise, it would go past a point of no return for him to be able to help.

Edward nodded in agreement.

"My God, Ed, what the hell happened?" Abi asked.

"I didn't do anything, Abigail. I swear."

"Well, something happened. Melissa is dead!" she snapped back at him.

"You mean my wife is dead," Edward replied, before breaking down into tears.

Deegan shot Abi a stern look – which she interpreted as *keep probing.*

"Okay. You're right, you're right. My sister was your wife, but what happened?"

"I don't know. She came from work flustered and panicked. She wouldn't say why. But she seemed detached, you know? Not herself at all."

"Did she say anything?" Abi pressed.

"Not really. I gathered something happened at work, but couldn't get it out of her. Next thing I know, she is lying on the floor and I am standing over her," Edward continued.

"What did you do?"

"Nothing, I swear. But I blacked out... that window in time is completely blank." He wept.

Deegan scoffed at the statement.

"Ed, what do you remember just before your blackout?" Abi asked again.

"Nothing. Just a strange noise. Almost like a droning, then nothing."

Deegan wasn't buying it and signalled to Abi to wrap it up, but she felt they were getting somewhere and begged Edward to elaborate on the noise.

"It was intense..."

"Go on."

"I can't remember everything," he snapped, "I think I had a migraine."

"From the noise?"

"I think so. I can't be sure. It was all a daze..." he replied, explaining that he didn't feel himself moments before blacking out. But when he came back round, his head felt crystal clear.

Edward tried his hardest to remember with flashes drip feeding back into his memory. His only explanation was an out of body experience and how he watched his hands wrap around Melissa's neck, squeezing and choking until her lifeless body collapsed onto the floor in front of him. "That's it, I remember now. It was the noise!" Edward shouted. "It triggered me. That fucking sound took over me. It controlled me and *they* made me do whatever they wanted me to do."

"Who did? Who's they?" Abi said, clearly startled by his sudden eagerness.

"I don't know. The people who operate those new aerials!" Edward shouted, almost becoming hysterical.

Deegan had heard enough and stood up from the table. "The interview is over. Christ, this was a waste of time."

"No, wait, he's telling the truth," Abi begged.

"He's insane!" Deegan shouted as he turned for the door to summon guards to take the suspect back to his holding cell. But in the split-second he let his guard down, Edward lunged forward and somehow whipped a firearm from Deegan's holster.

Edward pulled the hammer back and pointed the gun, shouting, "Stay back. Stay the fuck away from me!" as he backed himself into the corner of the room.

"Ed, please," Abi pleaded, "think about what you're doing. You're going to get yourself killed."

"I'm already dead, Abigail. Don't you get it? They're in my head. They can make me do whatever they want me to do."

"Who can? Ed, you're just overwhelmed. Please, put the gun down and let's talk about this."

Armed guards lined up in the doorway, waiting to burst in and take him out. Deegan held his hands up and slowly moved towards the door.

"It's happening again, Abigail. The noise, it's coming back!"

"What noise? I can't hear anything." Abi shouted, trying her hardest to get him to calm down. "Everything is going to be okay, Ed. Trust me."

"There is only one way out of this nightmare, Abi. I'm sorry," he said as he raised the gun and pointed it at her. "I'm so sorry. But I can't let them win." Then he rammed the barrel of the gun into the roof of his mouth.

"No!" Abi screamed, but it was no use, the sound of his skull popping open reverberated in her ears, the sight of the blood and brain splattering across the walls and ceiling turned her stomach. Deegan acted quickly, shielding her eyes from the horrific scene as he pulled her out of the room. For the second time in two days, she fainted.

A low winter sun disappeared behind grey cloud as day entered night. Abi was recovering from fainting in the police station. On the side of her head, a large lump swelled and throbbed. As distracting as it was, it wasn't enough for her to forget the whirlwind couple of days that she had just lived through. But despite grief and confusion eating away at her, she couldn't bury the burning desire to know what had happened to her sister.

The guard in reception handed her a bottle of water, which she wasted no time uncapping and guzzling down, then proceeded to wipe the dribbles away from the side of her mouth. Without saying goodbye, she left the station, entered her car and checked her phone in the hope of an email reply from Shane. *Why the fuck did we only have one phone?* she moaned to herself, but supposed that they could never have planned for a situation like this before.

The phone failed to connect, and she punched the steering wheel in frustration. What was the deal with the signal around here? With nowhere to go and with no way of contacting Shane, she decided a drive home was needed, just to check-in, regroup and then try and get answers from there.

Abi's concentration was broken by the sound of knuckles tapping against the passenger window. Startled, she turned her head to see a young woman signalling to her. She'd tried to ignore her, but the woman persisted and kept beckoning to her to open the window.

"Call I help you?" Abi called through a slit in the glass.

"You're Melissa's sister, aren't you? Abigail, right?"

"Who wants to know?"

"I do. My name is Lucy Ward. I'm a friend of hers," the woman answered, nervously looking around to see if she was overheard.

Abi took a minute; her mind was swimming with a million thoughts. "She's never mentioned you to me before."

"Please, can I come in or can we go somewhere where we can talk? I have some important information that might be of interest to you," Lucy insisted.

Abi looked around cautiously. Lucy appeared to be alone, almost in a state of distress. Her red hair was unkempt, unwashed and hung down around her shoulders. Her clothes looked like they hadn't been changed or washed in days and her eyes stared into the car, wide and owl-like. With the flick of a switch, Abi unlocked the passenger door, allowing her to sit in the car. Trusting her gut instinct was all she had to go on.

"Okay, Lucy, tell me, what's this 'important information'."

"I will. But, let's drive away from these aerials and find somewhere we can talk."

"The aerials?"

"Yeah, I'll explain more later. We haven't got much time. They'll know we are here."

Abi looked at her in disbelief. She wanted answers about her sister's demise, not to talk about aerials. "Seriously? No. Tell me about my sister. You said you were her friend? Then how come I've never heard of you?"

"We worked together on the same project at Ziegler. Outside of the office we weren't allowed to talk about it... they even made us sign non-disclosure agreements."

Abi assessed the strange woman sitting next to her and struggled to work out whether she was telling the truth. She certainly wasn't acting as weird as old man Arthur or the hotel receptionist.

"I've said too much," Lucy continued, "please, let's get away from the aerials and I'll explain everything. I promise."

Abi trusted her gut, turned the key in the ignition, backed out of the car park and headed north along the coast road.

The journey north took over two hours. Lucy didn't say anything else until they were clear of the last aerial that was dotted along the road. With so much going on, Abi hadn't noticed they were over the border in Northern Ireland.

Lucy smiled and muttered, "Good thing they haven't expanded into the UK. Yet..."

"What? Who hasn't? Can we discuss this madness? I'm miles from home, my sister and her husband are dead. What the fuck is going on here?" Abi asked, growing angry.

"Okay, okay. Calm down. I just had to be sure we were safe."

"From who?"

"Just pull over. Here is fine..."

Abi pulled over the car and listened to Lucy's story. She explained that Ziegler were not who they said they were and what she and Melissa had worked on was not what they thought it was. In the beginning, they'd been hired on temporary contracts as support staff, a low-level tech gig to get themselves valuable work experience. Everything seemed fine. Money was decent and they both were based in a nice modern office in Dublin City. But as the months went by, the support calls stopped coming in and management became more secretive about the project. At a performance review, they both chanced their arm and asked for more money – which was granted without question. They didn't complain.

"So, what happened the night before my sister died?" Abi asked. "She tried to call me."

"I'm getting to that. We were happy to plod along, easy work and good pay. Who wouldn't want that, right?"

"Sure..."

"Well not your sister. She started hassling the management team about wanting to attend the team meetings. Career-girl talk, showing ambition, looks good to the company, right?"

"I guess," Abi answered.

"Well not for Ziegler..."

Lucy explained that Melissa's lack of career progression was starting to get to her, especially when the pair of them had to repeat the mundane act of clocking in for a nine to five shift that involved nothing.

"Don't you see, Abi? It was a front. Something to make them look legitimate for when the auditors came knocking."

"I don't follow. What were they covering up?"

"That's what Melissa found out. The project was disguised in the media as a national upgrade to the data network. You know, turbo speed broadband for everyone, everywhere."

Abi nodded. That much she was aware of at the very least.

"But," Lucy continued, "that's not what the aerials are at all. Melissa hatched a plan to crash one of the big meetings. She thought if she could pick up on some of the current threads and write a report, then she could dazzle the bosses without them seeing her coming. She'd even planned to have a presentation ready to go and boasted to me about how she was going to make radical changes that would be better for the company... and her career, of course."

"She never made it to any of the meetings, did she?" Abi asked.

"Actually, she did, but the management team were having a presentation of their own. So, she stole one of the guest attendance badges and sat at the back," Lucy continued, again looking around nervously in case someone was listening.

"You're fine. What did she learn?" Abi pressed.

"The aerials. They can control people's minds. Like shepherds herding sheep. They want to control the population."

Abi looked at her in disbelief. "Get out of here! You expect me to believe this nonsense?"

"It's not nonsense. Melissa called me afterwards, she told me what I just told you. Only she was convinced she was being watched. 'They're in my head,' she kept repeating over and over."

Abi refused to believe it – no way could something so elaborate come into operation without anyone knowing. It had to be a conspiracy theory, a rumour. "And what about Edward?"

"My guess is, they got him to do their dirty work."

"Well, Lucy, your story would make a good film. I'll give you that," Abi said dismissively. "Why seek me out?"

"The last thing Melissa said to me before her call disconnected was to find you and tell you what happened."

"Why?"

"Because you know her personal passwords. She didn't want to tell me over the phone in case they were listening. She said if you could log me into her work computer, then I could steal the logs that the aerials transmit and we can go to the newspapers with the story."

"Her work computer? In the office in Dublin?"

"Yeah. Once we have the logs, we can prove that the management issued the commands that caused her death."

Abi sat in silence, pondering her potential actions. The plan seemed solid enough, but her head spun at how outlandish the whole day had been. At the same time, what had she to lose? Melissa and Edward were dead. If Lucy was crazy, the worst that would come of it would probably be a trespassing charge, though the fact Lucy had an access card went a long way to refuting that. But if

Lucy was telling the truth, then she couldn't let Melissa die for nothing, and they could put a stop to the aerials before the grid became fully operational.

The drive south towards Dublin seemed to take an age and Abi thought hard about everything as she tried to piece all of the events together. Grief-stricken over Melissa's loss as she was, she couldn't rest without finding answers, especially if Edward hadn't been responsible. Could she trust Lucy? She was a stranger after all... Her instincts drove her forward, and trusting Lucy had a big part to play in that decision.

They approached the city around midnight. Abi noticed that the aerials had not been erected on the tight and narrow streets. Perhaps they were here in another form? Or maybe the project hadn't reached the main urban districts yet? Either way, they had to try and expose what was happening.

After ditching the car a few blocks away, the duo approached the building cautiously. Lucy struggled with the swipe card reader on the door, while Abi kept watch. In both directions, the street was deserted. The sound of the city hummed off in the distance with a mix of traffic and people. Her concentration was broken from the sound of the reader approving Lucy's card. "Come on," she whispered.

Lucy led the way into the lift, selected the eighth floor and exhaled loudly as the doors closed behind them. "Are you nervous?" she said softly.

"A bit," Abi replied, "it all seems a little easy."

"At this time of night, there is no one here. My company rents this building and as part of the deal all staff required 24-hour access."

"I see."

The lift pinged, signalling their arrival. Together they emerged from the lift, Lucy leading the way through the corridors. "My office is just up here."

The door opened with a loud creak, fluorescent lights overhead struggled and blinked a few times before coming on. Abi was disappointed to see nothing more than a typical modern-day office. Beechwood tables, swivel chairs and a large window on the far side that overlooked the city.

"That's your sister's PC there," Lucy said, "come on, we need to be quick."

"Will logging in at this hour trigger any alarms or anything like that?" Abi asked.

"No, it'll be fine. Here's her log-in screen. Enter the password," Lucy asked, pushing herself away from the desk to allow Abi in.

Abi's mind went blank. Why would Melissa assume that she knew her password? She made two attempts, with no success. Abi rubbed her temples and muttered, "Think Abigail, think."

"We only get three attempts before the account locks," Lucy stated.

Then, like a lightbulb turning on, she had it. She remembered a dinner party a few months before. Abi and Shane hadn't wanted to go, but attended at Melissa's begging. On the night, Abi recalled Shane acting like a spoilt child who wanted to go home and, just like a frustrated mother with her infant in public, Abi gave him her phone to play with after dinner. His petulance was outstanding, but despite his carry on, an important piece of information grew clear in Abi's mind. Melissa's home Wi-Fi password. "Of course!" Abi shouted, delighted with the epiphany.

"What?" Lucy asked. "You think you got it?"

"I'd put my house on it being this..." Abi said and continued to input the series of letters and numbers into the password field – *T3llMyWif3iL0veH3r!*

The screen unlocked and Abi laughed at the result.

"You're joking me?" Lucy exclaimed.

"Ha, I knew it. She always joked about forcing Ed to type silly things so that he'd pay more attention to her and less on himself." Abi laughed, smiling at Melissa's personality shining from beyond the grave as she pushed herself out away from the desk, "Your turn to drive."

Lucy didn't hesitate, clicking and typing furiously at the workstation. She popped open Melissa's drawer, removed a USB key, popped it into the PC and began a large transfer of files. "Shouldn't take too long…"

"Step away from the computer!" a voice screamed from the doorway. The girls turned to see a man standing with a gun pointed straight at them.

"Inspector Deegan—," Abi began.

"Not one word, Abigail," he snapped. And it was at this point Abi noticed that he seemed different from when she'd left him that morning. His eyes looked sunken in, with large black bags beneath each of them. His weight seemed to have radically dropped in a short period of time and he spoke in a monotone. "I've been following you two. What you are doing is trespassing and theft of private property."

"But Daniel, I'm just collecting my sister's things," Abi chanced.

"You don't fool me. We know all about your plan."

"We?"

"Yes," Deegan stated, "now back away from that PC and place your hands above your head."

Abi stepped forward, blocking Deegan's view, while Lucy whipped the USB key from the PC and slyly slid it into her pocket. The inspector barked his orders again and warned them that if he had to order them again, he would open fire.

They complied.

Deegan marched the pair out to the corridor, standing them up against the wall. From his pocket, he removed two pairs of zip ties and proceeded to bind the girl' arms behind their backs.

"What's going on here, Daniel?" Abi shouted, "this isn't normal procedure!"

Lucy turned to Abi, her eyes tear-filled and sad, "It's over, Abigail. They caught us. And they are going to make us disappear."

"What are you talking about?"

"The logs on the PC. The aerials? They're everywhere. The company, the government, it's all a conspiracy and they eliminate everyone who learns the truth."

"Time to shut up now," Deegan interrupted.

"Don't tell me to shut up!" Lucy barked back, but quickly found herself lying on the ground struggling to catch her breath.

Abi stared in shock at Deegan as he raised his fist to her, almost daring her to speak so she'd receive the same shot to the stomach. Her mind raced. It all seemed like a bad dream. How could this be happening? *A fucking zombie nation.*

Abi was seconds from admitting defeat when something down the corridor caught her attention – *the USB key* – Lucy had removed it from her pocked and tossed it down the hall.

"Quick Abi. Grab it and get out of here!" Lucy screamed.

Abi froze on the spot and watched Lucy spring to her feet and swiftly kick Deegan between the legs. The inspector moaned in pain as he dropped to his knees. Lucy screamed for Abi to go once again before lunging at Deegan and sinking her teeth into his neck, causing him to wail in agony.

Abi didn't hesitate. She took off down the hall, stopping to drop onto her knees and try to scoop up the key. Unable to see it, she couldn't master her balance and kept fumbling about, while behind her Lucy continued biting.

Abi managed to catch the key between her fingers, and without looking back made her way around the corner to the lift. Using her nose and tongue, she summoned the elevator. She watched the counter above the door as it slowly made its way up to their floor. From around the corner, screams echoed.

A chime went off above the door and the lift opened, inviting Abi to jump inside. As she did, a gunshot echoed from around the corner. She screamed and pressed her back to the panel, frantically pressing the button for the ground floor. "Please close. Please, please."

The doors began to close, but when they got halfway, they shot back open. Probably an oversensitive sensor being triggered. She pressed the button again furiously.

Down the corridor, Deegan shouted, "Abigail. Oh, Abigail. There is no escape. Once we all join them, the world will be a better place."

The doors began to close again and Deegan appeared on the other side. He raised his gun and pointed it at Abi. She screamed in terror and jumped to the side. The gun fired, the bullet whizzed through the doors as they slammed shut, the impact shattering the mirror and causing shards of glass and splinters to rain down on Abi as she crouched and faced downward.

The doors opened and she spilled out onto the ground floor. The coast was clear, for now. She had to think fast. Rolling onto her back, she grabbed hold of a large piece of the shattered mirror. Her feet wedged the door open to prevent Deegan from summoning the lift, then she shifted onto her side and proceeded to cut into the cable tie. It was a tricky process, but after what seemed liked forever, she managed to get her wrists free.

Abi went straight for the exit, but as she grabbed hold of the handle, the monotone voice called from behind her.

"Abigail," Deegan called, "you need to come with me."

She turned to look into his dull eyes. "I'm not going anywhere with you."

"What's the plan, Abigail? You get out of the city? Contact the newspapers? Is that it? I'm afraid at this point, there is no going back. We are everywhere."

"Who's we?" Abi begged – terrified by the pistol locked on her – her words echoing high above to the balconies that overlooked the lobby.

"We are united. We are control. The system is live and cannot be stopped."

"The project?"

"Yes."

"Melissa tried to stop it going live, didn't she?" Abi asked.

"I don't know about that. All I know is, we command the aerials and together we all achieve... the perfect utopia. Like a colony of bees. Busy, hard working all for the one common goal."

"Fucking slaves! That's all that has been achieved here," Abi barked.

"We are freer now than we ever were before, Abigail. Now come with me," Deegan proclaimed. He stepped forward – holding his gun on her – and beckoned her to come and kneel before him.

Abi resigned herself to defeat. What other choice did she have? The lunatic could fire at any second and then the truth would never be free. But what would happen if she went with him? Would her mind be corrupted like his? Would she be assimilated into this brain hacking regime?

"Turn around," Deegan ordered as he removed a pair of handcuffs from his belt.

Abi, terrified, obliged. She wanted to cry and wished for this nightmare to end as she waited for the steel to clamp down on her wrists. But the clamp never came, instead she heard gurgled cries. She turned and, to her surprise, he was on the ground clutching his neck – blood pouring from an open wound. Standing above him, a blood-drenched Lucy with a large shard of broken mirror in her hand.

"Oh my God!" Abi screamed in disbelief.

"Abi—" Lucy answered as she dropped to the floor.

Abi rushed to her aid and noticed that Lucy wasn't only covered in Deegan's blood, but was soaked with her own.

"Lucy—"

Lucy signalled to her to be quiet. "They can hear us. The aerials. Soon, the signal will be in everyone's head."

"Not us, Lucy. They can't get to us. We won't let them," Abi answered firmly.

"It's outside of our control, Abi. This is what your sister found out. The answers are right there in the logs on the USB key. Ziegler plan to implant their signal into everyone. The first phase was done through mobile phones. This broke the human mind down easier, allowing the signal to enter, consume and control. Melissa knew this and tried to blow the whistle. You live off the grid, which makes your mind harder to break down as you're not surrounded by signal-emitting technology."

"Lucy, this can't be—"

"It is and you're the only hope now. Take the USB key and get the data to a foreign agency. Get it outside the EU to the Americans or even the Chinese. Anyone who can—" Her words were interrupted by a violent cough. Her body convulsed, shuddered and she fought to catch her breath.

"Oh fuck, Lucy," Abi cried. She rose to her feet and ran over to the front desk. Emergency services were just a call away. Abi frantically grabbed the handset and raised it to her ear. She turned to look back at Lucy and to her horror, the girl was up on her knees, Deegan's gun in hand, raising it slowly.

"Put the phone down, Abigail. They'll hear you," Lucy said, her voice shifting into the familiar monotone.

"Not you too, Lucy?" Abi begged.

Lucy looked her dead in the eye, raised the gun, pointed it at her own temple – the sound triggering the building's alarm.

It took Abi a few seconds to comprehend what had happened. Lucy's body lay motionless on the floor, blood pumping from her head. The bullet had exited the other side and shattered the glass window on the front of the building.

Abi didn't have time to think, her instincts kicked in and she made haste for the door, down the street and into her car. The car struggled to life, slipped into gear and took off, leaving the deserted street in her rear-view mirror.

As she went beyond the city limits, she noticed the aerials dotted along the road. Lights blinked as they transmitted whatever it was that got inside of people's minds. Abi tossed her mobile phone out of the car window, pressed the accelerator and headed for home – she had to get Shane away from the aerial in front of the house.

Dawn broke to the sound of a murder of crows circling above her house. Light mist blanketed the fields and tarmac as she approached slowly. The house looked empty, no lights or signs of life anywhere along the countryside road.

Abi parked the car about a half-mile from the house, got out and slowly crept up. The aerial stood tall, blinking and signalling operation.

"Fuck!" Abi muttered to herself. "Please, Shane, tell me you're oblivious to all of this."

She hurried past the aerial, ran up the garden, unlocked the front door and entered the house. Everything seemed to be exactly as she'd left it – nothing out of place. She went to the bedroom to fetch her husband, her chest beating as she opened the door. Inside, the bed was made, never slept in and there was no sign of life anywhere in the room. She checked the en suite – nothing.

After checking the top floor, Abi searched the ground floor. At first, she didn't notice him in her hurry, but there he was – alive and well, drinking coffee in the kitchen.

"Shane, darling, are you okay?" she asked approaching him cautiously.

"That's the question I should be asking you? Where have you been?" he replied.

"You wouldn't believe me if I told you…"

"Try me."

"I know the truth about Melissa and that thing outside our house," Abi answered.

"You know nothing of it," Shane snapped, his voice suddenly shifting to the now-familiar monotone, almost robotic. He turned, dropping his coffee on the floor, his eyes dull and sunken.

"Oh no, my love. Not you as well?" Abi blurted out in horror at what stood before her. Her husband, one of those zombies.

"Yes, Abigail," he replied, revealing a revolver in his hand. "I know all about you and your sister. I even know about that device you carry in your pocket."

"How?"

"We are united. Interconnected and together as one. And because I love you, I'll give you a choice, hand over the device and join us or..." he said, raising the gun, the end of the barrel aimed straight at her.

"I can't do that, darling. Whoever these monsters are, they killed my sister. It's not right and now they're inside your head. Please, darling, please, use your mind, think past whatever hold they have on you. Let's out of here and get away. Please—"

"I can't..."

"Please, Shane. Be strong. I know you can do this," Abi begged as she watched her husband battle his inner thoughts. His eyes struggled to focus, his face crumpling as he tried desperately to break free from the aerial outside. Then, his eyes aligned and he was staring at Abi. "I love you, Abigail. But this ends now."

He lifted the revolver, pulled the trigger back and watched his wife plead for her life. In spite of everything, it was not enough. Whoever had control at the centre of the hive emitted the signal that took milliseconds to travel across the network, to the newly erected aerial outside of their home, pinging into his powerless mind.

As she hit the floor – the USB key sprung loose from her grip – the last thing she saw before her eyes closed was her husband taking a cigarette lighter to the little plastic device.

DOWN BELOW

Banished to his bedroom, Daniel McGovern was alone, crying in the dark. The burden of legacy is a mighty one, be it living up to the family name or struggling with the weight of parental expectation – it was something he struggled to cope with on a daily basis.

Outside the window, wind howled, while rain pelted the glass with relentless force. Wiping a tear from his eye, Daniel could not help but stare out into the night, wishing for an escape from the small village of Lusk.

His view overlooked the back garden. It was waterlogged from the back step to the small shed at the end of the path – raindrops echoing and chiming with unnatural rhythm as they pinged against its corrugated roof.

Beyond it, dim illumination from streetlights in the distance flickered as the storm continued to rage

– he found himself wondering about how he'd cope away from home, but quickly resigned himself to the fact that this was his life...

His concentration broke suddenly when something hit the back of his head. He turned quickly to see the culprit, and saw his little sister standing in his bedroom doorway, grinning cheekily from ear to ear, revealing her missing front teeth.

"Piss off, Jess!" Daniel roared. His warning fell on deaf ears, prompting Jess to pull another object from her pocket and take aim again.

"I mean it!"

A tennis ball shot across the room, narrowingly missing his head, spurring him to spring into action – the whole upstairs of the house rumbled from the galloping footsteps as he chased her across the landing.

Jess went to her room and tried to close the door, but was easily overpowered as her big brother forced his way in.

"Get out of my room! Mom? Dad? Get out!" she screamed in protest. But the words didn't stop her older brother pushing her to the ground. As he dragged her along the floor by her feet, roars from both parents filled the air for them to stop the horseplay.

Daniel silently signalled to his sister to be quiet, but she refused to stop screaming.

He was already in trouble and the last thing he wanted was for his father to come down on him again, as he was already grounded.

"Jess, stop it. Shut up! You're gonna get me in deep shit."

From downstairs, Hugh McGovern issued his last warning for the pair to stop messing around with one of those booming orders that made both kids stop in their tracks – they knew the next warning would not come in the form of stern words.

Daniel bent over to look Jess in the eyes. "You scream again and you're going into Dad's shed, you hear me? Ollie will get you."

It was the one threat that would always make her listen. The shed was a source of fear for the pair of them. Father used to say, *you better be good or you'll spend the night in the shed with Ollie!* For as long as they both could remember, Ollie had been a giant man-eating spider who lived in the shed and, even though Daniel was nearly sixteen, a little part of him was still wary of the shed.

Jess on the other hand, was petrified of spiders and always heeded her father's warning about the beat-up shack at the back of the garden. In her mind, it was a place that no one should ever enter. But the reality, of course, was that the shed was nothing more than a place for their father to store tools, a lawnmower and the wheelie bins...

Or was it?

"Ollie's not real. I'm nearly thirteen, you know. And I'm not afraid of make-believe things like that," Jess protested, trying to sound grown up but lacking any conviction in her statement.

Daniel didn't argue; in his mind she was one hundred percent right. He wanted to keep scaring her, but found it hard to keep up the game – especially when he was living in fear himself. In the end, their conflict was settled by a lingering silence and they both sat watching the rain – a rare moment of sibling truce.

The silence was broken when a noise erupted from the end of the garden; a loud squeal that could be heard over the rain clattering against the tin steel roof.

He turned to find Jess staring at him – a look of reassurance, much to his delight, she had heard it too. "It's your mind playing tricks on you. It was probably just the wind."

They listened carefully some more; the wind had slowed to a gentle breeze as the heavy rain began to ease.

Satisfied with his answer, Jess scrambled across the room and grabbed her iPad, then disappeared into the warm glow of her iPad screen.

Daniel watched her as her eyes turned zombie-like in the screen's light.

He envied her.

She always seemed to get away with murder and he wished Father would treat him the same way. But he had come to terms long ago with the fact that his dad must have had his favourite at this stage, so he'd just have to get on with it. *Get school out of the way and then move away from Fingal County once and for all.* That was his plan, anyway. It wasn't concrete, but gave him something to work towards.

The rain receded to a light drizzle that elegantly danced in the streetlights' haze. Daniel could feel his eyes getting heavy, and his sister was not far behind.

Time for bed.

Reaching across the bed to break her concentration, Daniel aimed for her shoulder, but before he could tap it, the strange noise bellowed again – this time a little louder, then it was followed by a loud moaning.

Jess dropped the iPad against her chest, her eyes wide. "That was not the wind!?"

Daniel found it hard to disagree, as the pair darted for the window...

Nothing stirred in the damp, dark garden below; it was eerily quiet.

"Ollie?" Jess whispered, with a hint of fear.

"It's just our minds playing tricks on us. Ollie isn't real, you said so yourself."

They peered out the window for a while longer, concluding that the noise was the work of their imaginations or indeed, it could have been the wind.

After they both got themselves into bed, the house began settling for the night.

The strange noise kept repeating in their heads...

Eventually, Daniel managed to force himself to sleep.

Jess plugged her ears with her iPad headphones. *Just another one of Dad's tales to scare us and keep us in line*, she told herself over and over again.

Ruth McGovern went to a great effort to serve up a big family dinner. Hugh sat at the head of the table, as always, and didn't thank her as his wife placed a plate of hot food in front of him. Instead, he was fixated on Jess and Daniel, observing their demeanour. He was a stern man and poor table manners were a pet peeve that could easily trigger his short temper.

The kids were quiet, picking silently at their food.

Ruth pottered around a little more before sitting at the opposite end of the table. With a shy smile she glanced up. "Enjoy, everyone." The quartet sat in silence, nibbling – listening to the cutlery clinking.

"Anyone going to tell us about their day?" Hugh said. His question went unanswered.

Ruth replied with a story about her trip to the supermarket – it was met with silence and the quiet clinking of cutlery returned.

"What about you two? What's going on? Any news?"

Daniel looked up from his plate to find Jess staring at him. He knew instantly what she wanted to say, but instead he opted for a shrug of the shoulders before looking down at his grub.

"Dad... Is Ollie, real?" Jess finally blurted out, her eyes not daring to look up from her plate.

Hugh took a moment to swallow what was in his mouth before glancing at Ruth, who knocked back a glass of wine in response.

"What was that, darling?" he asked, his voice sounding timid for the first time in ages.

"Ollie... You know. The monster in the shed?" Jess said, her eyes slowly lifting upward, wide with expression.

"Oh! Took me a moment there. Ha, the giant man-eating spider? Good memory, darling. But no, of course not. Don't be silly," Hugh replied.

The silence continued.

While they ate, Ruth appeared to venture off elsewhere in her mind. She stared out the window, drinking wine while her dinner went untouched and cold.

Both kids found themselves wondering why she was so absent. The sullen look on her face suggested something was on her mind.

Jess kicked Daniel under the table and, when he looked up at her, she nodded towards their mother. He responded with an eye roll.

"We heard him last night," Jess continued.

Her statement caught Ruth's lost attention. "What do you mean?" she asked.

Jess proceeded to tell her mother about the strange noises emitting from the shed, but before the story was fully finished, Ruth had pretty much consumed the full bottle of wine, then turned away as if all interest was suddenly lost – a regular occurrence at the McGovern dinner table these days.

"That's just an old story, darling," Hugh interrupted, returning with his trademark stern manner. "I only told you it when you were little, to scare you. Kids liked being scared... Now finish your greens and help your brother with the dishes."

A storm raged after dinner, but not outside. Instead it came from downstairs – Jess and Daniel listened to the confrontation taking place in the kitchen. The door was closed, so the exchange of words was faint to the children's ears, but they both figured it was over Mam's drinking again. They weren't sure when this problem had started, but Daniel was convinced it had been well over a year ago now. In fact, he found it hard to recall what she was like before the excessive boozing.

These arguments tended to end in the same way, with Daniel intervening on his mother's behalf, which in turn left him beaten, bruised and sent to his room.

To cool off, Hugh would take Jess and Ruth on a drive. When they came home, the family would go to bed while Hugh locked himself away in the shed – sometimes for hours at a time.

However, the usual pattern didn't play out the same way tonight. The shouting stopped, leaving Daniel in limbo about whether he should go down or not.

When his mother eventually left the kitchen, heading for bed, she left his enraged father pacing the kitchen.

Jess came into Daniel's room seeking comfort, and in typical big brother fashion, he wrapped his arm around her and held her. "Hopefully he'll leave us alone tonight."

The back door slammed with a force that shook every eave in the house.

The kids ran to the window and watched their father storm across the wet grass towards the end of the garden. In one hand, a set of keys glinted in the moonlight – in the other, a plastic bag.

It was hard to make out from the window, but as Hugh fiddled with the lock on the shed door the kids watched.

When door eventually opened, a light came on, revealing the white plastic bag and its contents – something deep red, bulging, dripping what appeared to be a red liquid onto the floor.

Hugh stood in the doorway, then turned around, his gaze fixated on the back of the house – both kids looking on, scared.

They could see he was taking deep breaths, almost as if he was gearing himself for something. His eyes were transfixed, intense, frightening Jess.

He flinched, then was out of sight. The light went out and the door slammed shut.

It was the one area of the McGovern household that was strictly off-limits to the children. When they were younger, it hadn't bothered them as they were both scared of the man-eating spider that lurked within. But as they grew older, they started noticing signs of odd comings and goings.

This raised questions about their father. Was the shed simply a place for housing tools, lawnmowers and the usual crap DYI-type dads liked to fill them with? Or was the secrecy justified? If there wasn't a giant man-eating spider in there, what was?

Hugh would often disappear into the shed after the kids went to bed, sometimes Daniel would lay awake wondering what was going on and as he got older, his curiosity grew. It was a pattern that was always there, as far as he was concerned, so he never felt a need to question it. Over time, he picked up on his father's secretive stance on the matter and some questions needed answering.

The McGovern children decided that the time had come to break down the psychological barrier that always kept them away. The blood dripping from the bag was confirmation that something was not right.

Daniel thought to himself, *normal dads don't do that. They work, come home, have a beer and watch football on TV... Don't they?*

"You know what? We're going to find out once and for all, what goes on inside that shed," Daniel announced. "This has been going on for too long."

"What about Ollie?" Jess asked.

"Jess, come on. You're twelve years old. There is no man-eating spider in our shed."

"You've never been in the shed. So, why the secret?" Jess questioned.

"Probably the same reason Mam is an alcoholic," Daniel replied with the assurance of an adult, and an all-knowing smirk.

"Poor Mom," Jess concluded.

"Explains all their fighting and her drinking doesn't it?" Daniel said. "In the morning, we'll pretend to go to school as normal, but after they leave for work, we'll find out once and for all. Fuck the rules! You with me?"

Jess hesitated, but agreed.

The kids left for school as usual, but took a detour into a laneway at the end of their street. They watched the house like hawks, waiting for both parents to leave. And when they did, they went back inside, searching for Hugh's spare set of keys.

It took all morning, but eventually, the keys were found in Hugh's bedside locker, hidden beneath a pile of old paperwork.

They had what they needed – time to investigate.

At the shed door, Daniel wrestled with the lock. The key struggled to turn, as the lock was stiff from being exposed to too many winters.

When it eventually popped open, a sudden rush of fear ran over them.

What lurked beyond the door? Was there a giant man-eating spider was lying in wait, with its big red eyes and long skeletal limbs ready to pounce on the kids as soon as they entered? At least that was what they had been told all of their life if they entered, and now finally, the moment had arrived for them both to charge in and face their childhood fear.

The door slammed shut behind them – leaving only a faint hint of sunlight creeping through the cracks. It was hard to see. Daniel ran his hand along the brick wall, finding the light switch. "You ready?" he called out in the dark to his sister.

"Yes, Dan. Turn it on now, please."

The bulb above where they stood came on with a harsh brightness that caused them both to squint. Startled, they rubbed their eyes as they struggled to focus.

Their blurred vision quickly cleared, and they could see everything around them.

The first thing that they noticed was obvious... There was no giant man-eating spider with big red eyes about to lunge forward and kill them. In fact, the roof, the walls and the whole shed were spotless – no signs of arachnid life at all – the bricks painted a pale grey. In one corner a yard brush and rake sat neatly. On the other side of the room stood a large bookcase with hundreds of plastic binders – all neatly labelled.

"What the fuck?" Daniel gasped.

He ran his finger along the spines, inspecting the titles. They looked like handwritten medical journals and other binders seemed to follow a common theme of surgery and diseases, all of which dated back at least fifteen to sixteen years.

The roof was insulated and when inside, you'd never tell there was a steel corrugated roof on top of it. A large black rubber mat sat in the centre of the floor.

"There is nothing in here?" Jess asked, her eyes wide with wonder.

"There has to be, are you telling me Dad is some sort of backyard doctor?" Daniel said condescendingly. "There's more to this place..."

"There's nothing but books in here, Daniel. Perhaps it is just his study area? You know, like the library in school," Jess replied.

Daniel felt a worrying unease creep though his body. He thought that they had overstepped their boundaries. First skipping school and then trespassing in the one place they were warned not to ever dare go. "Fuck this, come on, let's get out of here, I don't want Dad to catch me in here—"

As soon as Daniel said the words, he felt a thump against the soles of this feet.

Then another one.

Thump!

Jess felt it too. They looked at each other, didn't speak, but their eyes told each other everything they needed to know.

"Move!" Daniel ordered, while pushing Jess back against the bookcase. He reached down and grabbed a corner of the rug. He jerked it back, revealing a small steel hatch. Both sets of eyes grew wide with amazement at what they'd just discovered. It was circular in shape and had a large bolt holding it closed. It looked like something from an old war film. A bomb shelter? Access to the sewers? Whatever it was, it was a secret that Hugh didn't want anyone to know about. That much, they were sure of.

"What the fuck is this?" Daniel gasped.

Before his sister could reply, another loud thud came from beneath it. There was something moving down there – and judging by the sound, it was large.

Jess's thoughts shifted to the childhood warning, imagining a massive spider waiting for the latch to open so that it might jump out and catch its prey like something from *The Hobbit*.

Daniel bent down and grabbed the bolt.

"What are you doing?" Jess screamed.

"We have to check it out. Don't we?"

Jess froze with fear. A childhood phobia was about to be confronted and she wasn't sure if she was prepared for it.

"It's alright, Jess. We've passed the point of no return. It's probably more of his geeky journals," Daniel said, trying to reassure her.

"Journals and books don't hit things, Dan," she snapped, her voice filled with fear.

"Relax. I'm going to check it out. I have to know."

Jess braced herself as the bolt opened with a loud click.

Daniel lifted the hatch door and was instantly hit with a strange smell that wafted up into the air. It looked like the entrance to a sewer, a rusty steel ladder led the way down into what appeared to be a chamber. It was dark down there, but there was a faint light glowing, and unlike a sewer, it was bone dry.

Daniel positioned himself on top of the ladder and gave Jess a reassuring look that beckoned her to follow him down.

At the bottom, they were both surprised to find the chamber well insulated, in fact it resembled a small trendy apartment more than anything. The floor was carpeted and the walls were covered in wallpaper that had a vintage feel to it. The air was warm and as they stepped out into the middle of the dwelling, the size of the space surprised them.

Why did Hugh keep this place a secret?

Multiple thoughts flowed through their minds as they moved about, taking it all in. But at the end of the room, something caught Daniel's eye that immediately raised an alarm – a bed, but not a normal bed. He could not help but think it looked like something straight from a mental hospital. Silver steel frame upon black rubber wheels and restraints for a person's limbs. Beyond the bed stood another bookcase full of journals and what appeared to be Tupperware boxes. On close inspection they seemed to be full of some sort of medical equipment.

"That's a weird bed," Jess remarked.

Daniel didn't reply, instead he ran his hand over the mattress. It was warm to touch. *Had someone been sleeping here today?* In the corner of the room, there was a section tiled off, creating a small walk-in shower. And that's when he noticed a shower head, still dripping, and beads of condensation slowly evaporating from the ends of the shower curtain.

From the other side of the room, a strange groan echoed, sending a chill up the siblings' spines. They were not alone in the room and whatever it was behind them, it was hiding in the shadows looking straight at them.

"Who are you?" Jess asked, slowly turning to try and make out who or what the figure was, but all she could see was a silhouette standing there, silent.

The shadowy figure caused them both to freeze and they could do nothing else but watch as it slowly swayed from side to side, with the odd nervous twitch thrown in.

"Who are you?" The shadow spoke with a voice that eerily sounded like Daniel's.

"I asked you first," Jess replied.

"No, I asked you first," it responded, leaning forward slowly.

Daniel suddenly felt he wasn't afraid anymore. He took a step forward towards the shadow and held out his hand in a friendly gesture. "I'm Daniel."

The figure's hand emerged from the shadow revealing a dark green skin colour and finger nails that had been chewed to a bloody stub. The sight caused Jess to recoil with disgust, but Daniel offered his hand in friendship anyway.

The shadow clamped its hand down hard on Daniel's, squeezing tightly and then its face emerged from the shadow. "I'm Daniel!" it said, almost mocking the tone in Daniel's voice.

The brief sight of the shadow's face caused Daniel to gasp loudly, but before he fully registered what he was seeing, the shadow pulled him towards it and then kicked Daniel hard in the chest, sending him sprawling across the room – it then stood out, revealing its full body. Skin, green, sick-like, and it spat at Daniel.

"The Monster!" screamed Jess, but before she could register anything, it had darted to the other side of the room, rapidly ascending the ladder.

Jess ran to Daniel, who lay on the floor struggling to catch his breath and in a state of shock. "What was that, Dan?"

Daniel struggled to find the words, but eventually blurted out, "I don't know..."

The pair gathered themselves and made their way over the ladder. Looking up to the hatch door, they could see the sunlight illuminating the inside of the shed. Daniel mumbled away to himself and Jess tried her hardest to decipher what he was saying, eventually giving up.

When they emerged from the shed, Hugh stood with a menacing pose. His eyes locked on them. "What were you doing in my shed?" he screamed at them.

Jess tried to defuse his anger using her *Daddy's Girl* sweet talk angle, "I'm sorry Daddy, we heard noises and—"

"Aren't you in enough trouble already, Daniel?" Hugh shouted, ignoring his daughter's attempt to distract him – his aggression turning towards his son.

"We are very disappointed in you," said Ruth, who appeared from behind her husband, sullen and weak-looking.

Both parents entered the shed and saw that the hatch was open. They glanced at each other and mouthed the words, *Oh fuck.*

With haste, they turned and ran back to the house – dragging the kids with them.

In the kitchen, both Daniel and Jess stood in bewilderment at the flurry of motion that rebounded around the room. Hugh locked all the windows, doors and shouted orders at Ruth along the way. The room fell silent when he returned and for the first time, Daniel saw a genuine fear in his father's eyes.

Hugh looked at him, his shoulders hung low, almost defeated. "It's the day we've dreaded for years, son. All thanks to you."

"It's the result of Seiðr..." Hugh announced to his family as they all gathered around the dining room table. No one said a word as they all stared blankly at him. He arranged himself at the head of the table, prepping them for the task on hand – the whirlwind of information overwhelming the children. It was as if all of this was rehearsed. Maybe, Hugh was right and it was the day that they all had dreaded?

"Who was that in the basement?" Daniel asked.

"And what is Seiðr?" Jess asked with innocent curiosity.

Hugh took a moment, thinking to himself, *the kids are not stupid and it's time to tell them. Surely, now is the time?*

He looked to Ruth for approval, but she could barely muster up a smile from her weary face.

"I'm sorry, son," Hugh began, "your mother and I have not been entirely truthful to you. Or your sister."

"What is it, Dad? We have a right to know what's going on," Daniel asked with a hint of fear hidden deep within his tone.

"Seiðr is an artform I applied to my work."

"What?" Jess asked again.

"It was supposed to be about, err, life. But my work and research has meandered over the last few years. Never in a million years did I expect things to unfold the way that they have..." he said, before trailing off into mumbling.

With a nod and a deep breath, Hugh finally committed to the situation and disclosed everything. Once the initial words came out, everything else flowed with ease. At the core of the project lay a cold hard truth. A family secret that had lain buried in the back garden since the day Daniel was born.

"Danny, you have a twin brother."

The news rebounded within Daniel's head like a pinball jacked up on amphetamines. He looked at every face around the table and hoped that this was all some sort of elaborate joke. A wisecrack to get him back for the trouble he'd been getting into. But, as the silence continued, the realisation of the truth began to sink in. He *did* have a twin.

"My brother?"

"Yes, son. I'm sorry you had to find out this way," Hugh answered.

Daniel stood up, stumbling back from the table. "You guys are messing with me? Aren't you? Please, tell me you're messing with me?"

"I'm afraid not, Daniel," Hugh replied, rising slowly to look him in the eyes.

Ruth ran to console her son, her arms wrapping around him in a loving embrace. But Daniel rejected her with a shrug, continuing to protest the news. Eventually, he succumbed to her hug.

Jess ran to join them.

"Go on, Hugh. Tell them everything," Ruth demanded, her breath reeking from booze.

With a deep sigh, Hugh reached for a bottle of brandy that sat up on the top shelf of a cabinet in the corner of the room. He didn't bother with a glass, instead opting to swig a few large mouthfuls straight from the bottle before continuing. He then plucked up the courage to tell the kids about the day Daniel was born.

He explained that Daniel was one of a pair of conjoined twins; the other, they'd named Oliver. But their birth was not a usual one. The doctors had to perform an emergency separation in order to save the life of one of the infants. Oliver died shortly afterward, leaving Ruth in a complete state of despair and overwhelming grief.

Hugh remembered thinking, *a parent should never have to bury their child.*

On the day of Oliver's funeral, the heartbreak was almost too much for Ruth to take. It was pouring rain. The kind of rain that brought a chill with it. Despite this, she refused to leave the graveside, weeping uncontrollably as dirt filled in the hole. When Hugh eventually got her home, she was a shadow of her former self and part of her soul was in that grave with Oliver. So, wine became her only companion – this hurt Hugh more than anything. He tried everything to get her back on track. But none of the support services or therapy sessions could assist Ruth with her grief.

In the end, Daniel and his baby sister went to live with their auntie for a while, so Hugh could focus his efforts on his wife. It was the most challenging time in the family's history.

One day, Hugh reached his breaking point. He took Ruth to the emergency department of a psychiatric hospital. Ruth didn't put up much of a fight and just slept while they were waiting to be assessed. When the doctor eventually saw them, Hugh was ready to run out the door and leave her behind, but despite his desire to do just that, he held firm and comforted her during the assessment. The doctor asked all the usual questions and focused primarily on her depression and grief. It didn't take long for a decision to be made and she was admitted later that evening.

Hugh felt his world come to an end.

The hospital was located in Portrane – a part of the county Hugh was not familiar with, but this didn't stop him finding a local pub and proceed to drown his sorrows – and drown them, he did. But despite his drunken state, he met a man. A man who was willing to wrap his arm around him and counsel him over another pint of stout. Hugh didn't remember much about what was said that night, but he did remember when the conversation about grief and loss turned into a discussion with intrigue and hope. And from there he became aware of Seiðr.

Daniel and Jess looked at each other and then turned their attention to their mother, who sauntered over to the bottle of brandy and proceeded to drink from it. All the while, refusing to break a stare she had fixated on Hugh.

"Seiðr?" Daniel asked in disbelief, "What the fuck is that?"

"Watch your language!" Ruth barked as she plonked herself down at the table.

"Yes, son. That's what the man that night called it... it's a dark art used since the Norsemen came to Fingal," Hugh replied. "I didn't believe him at first. Thought it was nothing more than the ramblings of a drunken man. But son, he was telling the truth!"

"It's true, Danny. It's all true," Ruth added, almost weeping.

Daniel refused to believe that *the monster* in the shed was in fact, his brother. And not only a sibling he never knew about, but a reanimated one at that. It was too much information for him to process there and then. Before he could take in anymore, the room began to spin. Next, he hit the floor.

Through the dizziness, his parents tried to revive him, but he could barely register his father's fingers clicking with a snapping sound in front of his face and the cries of his mother who tried desperately to coax him out of his state of flux – but it was no use. The truth swirled around his mind like a hurricane. His thoughts raged out of control as the reality of the situation sank in, and bit by bit he edged closer to a total blackout.

Ollie the giant spider was real, but not in the form he and Jess had envisioned. Instead he was just a boy. One who was resurrected to combat his parent's unwillingness to commit to grief, and as time went by, the reality of their actions became clear.

Ollie's body was alive, his mind, however, was not. The boy's mind was dark, unpure from necromancy. Ollie was wicked and, at only nineteen months old, showed extreme behaviour which gravitated towards violence.

It didn't take long for his parents to take action.

Beneath the shed, Hugh constructed an underground shelter, which was converted into a living space. A small, but clean space in which Ollie would have to be kept, and for sixteen long years, the boy lived there without seeing the light of day.

"He can't be far. He's never been more than a few feet outside of the shed, he wouldn't know where to go!" Ruth stated as the family put their coats on in the hallway. The plan was simple: split up and search the village, catch Oliver, and bring him back to his domicile.

"You never know, Ruth. Lusk may seem small to us, but it is a vast unexplored world for someone like

Ollie," Hugh replied. "We need to act fast and get him back here. There is no telling what he could do out there."

The family split into three groups.

Hugh would head down the street towards the park. Ruth and Jess would canvas the doors and Daniel would stay behind to watch the house.

"If anything out of the ordinary happens, you'll call me straight away!" Hugh ordered his son.

Daniel nodded. On the outside he looked confident and in control, but inside his heart was palpitating with furious speed. His mother kissed him on the forehead before leaving, her breath still reeking of booze, and he thought to himself: *none of the neighbours will want to deal with this drunk.* Then he watched them walk to the end of the street and go their separate ways. His eager eyes were watching and hoping for Jess to turn around and make a silly face, but she never did.

Perhaps she is overwhelmed by the whole situation?

It didn't matter now because whatever Daniel felt suddenly compacted and intensified when the front door closed. His family home felt like a wide-open space and he felt vulnerable in it.

With haste, Daniel set off around the house, double-checking all the exterior doors and windows, making sure that everything was locked.

Once satisfied, he returned to the hall and sat on the foot of the stairs, armed with a baseball bat. His inner fears were consuming his mind as a black wave washed over him. A sharp chill ran up his spine, triggering a shudder in his shoulders – it was almost as if someone or something was breathing on the back of his neck. An unwanted presence. But, despite the crippling fear, a moment of clarity shone through. With a deep breath, he lifted his head and scanned the hallway.

Beyond the front door, a wind howled, announcing the arrival of the expected storm. Beside the door were two clear glass panes. Rain relentlessly pelted against them and with a flash, a bolt of lightning lit up the hall, followed closely by a clap of thunder. He worried about his family being caught out in the storm, his mother and sister especially. Hopefully they were in a neighbour's house waiting for a break in the rain. His father could be anywhere and this didn't really bother him too much. Then there was Oliver. His twin brother. Hidden beneath the earth for years. Why couldn't they grieve like normal people and move on? Bringing him back for a life of imprisonment was not the way.

Worry returned to his mind and with his senses kicking in, he called out with a raw dry throat, "You're here, aren't you?"

As soon as the last word left his mouth, the silence hit him harder than the rolling thunder outside.

His loneliness was broken.

"Yes, Daniel. I'm here. I never left," Oliver said as he emerged from the shadows in the hall. His skin, sickly green, his hair, long, matted, tossed over to one side. His eyes harboured pain, his teeth were gapped, crooked and yellow. Despite his awful appearance, it was the smell that demanded Daniel's attention the most – layers of unwashed and decaying skin. Rotting and foul. "Why would I leave, Daniel? This is my home... brother."

"I suppose I should welcome you, then?"

"Isn't that what families do when a loved one returns home?" Oliver replied, his voice crackling with a high-pitched squeak – clearly suffering the effects from the lack of interacting with the outside world.

He took a step closer, staring into Daniel's eyes. The closer he got, the more Daniel could see the sorry state the boy was in. "You – You're a monster."

"Am I, Daniel? Am I really? What would you know about monsters?" Oliver snapped back, his curious tone laced with slight aggression. "The only monsters here are the people who stood by and let

Father do the things he did to me and say nothing. They're the real monsters!"

"What things? What happened to you?" Daniel asked almost defensively.

Oliver leaned forward and grabbed Daniel by the wrist, his ailing skin cold against his twin's. Daniel tried to wriggle free, but Oliver refused and a struggle ensued. His other hand had a grip on the bat and with all of his might, Daniel wormed it free, swinging it at his brother.

Oliver intercepted with ease, displaying surprising strength, tossing the bat to one side. His fortitude was far superior to Daniel's and with little effort, he picked his brother up from the step, slamming him to the ground, which was followed by a swift kick to the gut, sending Daniel's limp body crashing against the front door.

"The only way to tell you what happened to me, is to show you what happened to me," Oliver said as he towered him.

Daniel looked up in horror at his brother's menacing glare, warm drool creeping through a gap in his teeth. And before he knew it, he was being dragged through the house by his hair.

Daniel screamed in pain and tried desperately to get loose, but Oliver held firm and lashed out punches and kicks in retaliation, subduing Daniel's weak efforts.

The backdoor burst open, allowing gusts of wind and rain to rush in. The elements pounded against Daniel's face. Beaten and bruised, he struggled against the disorientation.

Oliver had hit him hard, his face swelling instantly. From beneath the throbbing pain, he caught a glimpse of the garden shed.

Oliver, picking up the pace now, was not letting go, no matter what Daniel tried.

"Stop, Ollie! Please," Daniel cried.

"Shut up! You will see the world I grew up in and you'll see what Father has done, time and time again."

Before Daniel could respond, he felt his body lift from the ground. The sky flashed, thunder clapped, and his body – acting like a battering ram – crashed through the shed door. Daniel's body curled up in a heap beside the hatch entrance. He struggled to get his bearings and before he knew it, he was falling down the shaft, Oliver's foot the last thing he saw before he landed hard at the bottom.

He looked up, desperately begging for someone to come to the rescue, but all that was above was the sight of Oliver climbing down the ladder and the hatch door slamming shut behind him.

Deep within his slumber, Daniel struggled to return to the light. Whatever had hit him over the head must have been hard. His eyes cracked ever so slightly open, his vision blurring from the overhead lighting in the room. He could not make anything out but he knew exactly where he was. The bed he'd discovered earlier with Jess was beneath him, thick leather restraints secured his limbs to it. As his vision became clearer, Daniel's heart began to pound. Sweat poured from his forehead, rolling down, stinging his eyes – leaving him with no choice but to try and wipe them against his shoulder. But this was ineffective as it only added to the rawness and the burning sensation intensified.

His body ached all over.

With a scream, he called out for his mother...

From somewhere in the room, he could hear a creepy snigger, leaving him no choice but to release a whimper.

"We don't have much time," Oliver said as he slowly revealed himself from the shadows in the corner of the room, "and I need to give you a taste of what my life was like for all the years I lay on that very bed."

"Please, Ollie. Don't do this," Daniel begged.

Oliver brushed off his pleas as he worked his way around the room, lighting candles which created a menacing ambience.

For sixteen long years, Oliver had existed in this room. He never got to ride a bike, go to school or even experience the thrill of opening presents on Christmas morning. No, he lived here, alone. And with only one visitor a week – his father – to keep him alive.

Hugh was an angry man. People granted him it on the grounds of grief, but little did people know that his grief had manifested itself into something more; something disturbing, almost lustful in his relentless hunt to control life. And this was Oliver's plan, one he'd waited over a decade to get the chance to fulfil.

Beside the bed, there was a cart covered with a sheepskin blanket. Daniel listened to Oliver in horror as he told him that beneath the tarp, a set of tools were ready to go. The same tools that Hugh used for years to deliver Oliver his treatment – tools he called, *Daddy's Favourites*.

"The treatment, Daniel. That was his favourite thing. He'd get very excited about these tools and things he could do to me with them. Make me pure and rid me of my evil," Oliver explained.

"Evil? You're not evil. You're just a bit confused with the way things work in the real world. I can help you," Daniel begged.

"You can't help me."

With a quick snap of his wrist, Oliver whipped the blanket off the cart revealing Hugh's ritualistic instruments.

It took Daniel a few moments to realise what he was looking at. In his thoughts, he'd expected a set of tools made of steel or syringes – stereotypical instruments a doctor had at his disposal before a big surgery. But the longer he stared at them, the quicker the truth now became apparent. Everything Hugh had told him was a fabrication – an untruth designed to hide the deepest, darkest, family secret of all.

"That's right, Daniel. Look at them. I was resurrected by some pagan ritual... But not to live life... No. I was just the one he chose to use for his sick experiments. Now it is your turn to experience the treatment."

Hugh's treatment seemed to be nothing more than an exercise in sadistic pleasure. Sat on top of the cart was a mix of strange implements and BDSM toys. Oliver picked up one of the steel instruments and showed it to Daniel, "This was his favourite. He called it the tunnel dragger..."

Daniel struggled against his bounds, but it was futile. He screamed and warned his brother not to come near him, but Oliver could not be deterred. In one hand he held the dildo-like object and in the other, a pair of scissors. "Let's remove those pants, shall we?"

With a sharp incision, Oliver cut down from the waistline and once the tear was big enough, he forced the pants open with his hands, revealing Daniel's bare skin.

"Please Ollie, please. Don't do this to me! I know you're a little fucked up right now. But we can get you some professional help. It doesn't have to be like this."

"No! It's only fair, Daniel. It was this way for years. He used me to arouse sick men. Now you'll feel what I felt," Oliver replied as he prepared to ram the cold steel device into his brother.

Daniel squirmed and bit down hard on the pillow in anticipation of the impending horror... but the pain never came.

Instead, he heard a floorboard creak, forcing him to look for the origin of the sound. Like an assassin, Ruth had crept up on Oliver and seconds later, Daniel heard an almighty *thump*.

Next, he saw Oliver hit the ground, eyes glazed, unconscious, with a trickle of blood oozing from the side of his head.

Ruth frantically tried to release Daniel from his bounds, eventually succeeding. She didn't say anything, instead she just held him in a loving clutch. He squeezed back, thanking her, but the loving moment didn't last long as the scraping sound of the bat along the floor demanded their immediate attention. They both turned, expecting to see Oliver standing there, armed and ready to retaliate, but he was still laying unconscious on the floor.

Instead, there stood Hugh. His eyes were fired up with anger and his hands gripped tightly around the bat. "Step aside, Ruth," he ordered.

"Dad, what are you doing?" Daniel screamed.

"Something I should have done years ago," Hugh answered while staring at Oliver on the ground. He raised the bat above his head, stepped forward, ready to unload furious rage, regret and remorse. But before he could swing the bat in a downward motion, Daniel stepped in front of him and took the first blow firmly on the top of his shoulder – screaming in agony as a result.

Ruth ran to comfort her stricken boy.

The reality of her husband's actions became clear in her mind. She cradled Daniel, shielding him the best she could, but Daniel could not keep his mouth shut. "Please, Dad, don't hurt us anymore."

Hugh dropped the bat at the sight before his eyes. On the ground, one son lay unconscious, while the other begged for mercy. The sight of his son, and, his wife, wide-eyed and terrified at the man standing in front of her, sent a chill up his spine. His secret was out and if the authorities were informed, he would not be the head of the household for much longer.

Instead, he offered Daniel his hand and pulled the teen to his feet. With a hug, he assured him that Oliver would be allowed to leave the bunker beneath the shed – but it'd come at a small price.

His silence...

Three o'clock on Sunday evening was the traditional time slot for the McGovern's to sit down for their family dinner. Ruth normally spent the day slaving in the kitchen and usually cooked up a tasty roast. Honey glazed, with juices that would send any carnivore's taste buds into rapture.

The dining room table was set for four. Hugh positioned himself at the head of it so that he could oversee everything.

At the opposite end of the table sat Ruth, wiping the back of her arm against her forehead to clear remnants of sweat. To Hugh's right, Jess sat quietly staring at her plate, while on his left, Oliver sat nervously.

Hugh raised a glass of red wine, toasting them all.

Dinner was quiet.

The clinking and the scraping of cutlery against china chimed and sound tracked proceedings. Both Ruth and Jess ate silently and stared down at their plates, while Hugh was yet to touch his food, for he could not take his focus off Oliver. The boy was jerking and squirming in his seat, clearly uncomfortable with the situation. Hugh shouted at him for not holding his knife and fork correctly.

Oliver cowered with fear.

"No need to flinch, son. I'm not going to hurt you. Table manners are important and you must obey the rules. Isn't that right, family?"

Jess nodded and Ruth meekly replied, "Yes, of course, my love."

When dinner was concluded, dessert was offered, but no one wanted any. Instead, they continued to sit in silence, listening to Hugh ramble on about Lusk. It was his opinion that the council was just about housing anyone and everyone around them. Foreigners, criminals, and worst of all, paedophiles. And despite being that way inclined, he despised sex offenders. So, he subjected his family to another lecture on how his work was going to cure himself and other offenders of the *illness* they carried. He insisted that if he could get inside their mindset, then he could find a cure...

"Where is Daniel?" Jess interrupted, catching her father off-guard.

There was a long pause at the table. And one by one, they all turned to look at the head of the household. Hugh leaned over, placing his hand on Jess's shoulder. "Your brother is not well, little love. His behaviour has disrupted all of our lives."

"When is he coming home?" she asked, sheepishly.

Hugh replied by saying that Daniel would be coming home after he decided to change his attitude and be more like Oliver. Jess and Ruth didn't question him, instead they nodded with acknowledgement.

Oliver was a welcomed and obedient addition to the McGovern family and did everything he was told without question, and this made Hugh proud. Dinner concluded with him hugging his daughter. "Daniel wasn't revived by Seiðr, so it will take a little longer for his treatment to work. He'll be home soon and will be just like your brother... Oliver."

SEVEN YEARS GONE

On a cold Friday night in January, the last train departed. Onboard, passengers were nothing more than a few drunks and working professionals who refused to leave the office at a reasonable hour. The conductor, Adrian Ryan, did not mind all that much, as this was the shift where he could drink on the job and no one would know. In fact, it got to a point where he actually looked forward to working the late shift for this very reason, and while the train rattled along the dark tracks, he sat in silence alone in the cabin – a place for him to reflect on why his life was so unhappy. *Molly*. His wife of twenty years, missing the last seven – and he never got to say goodbye.

You see, his marriage to Molly was, for lack of a better word, chaotic. And his reasoning for it was money, or lack thereof. They struggled early on. He loved her, no doubt about that, but found it hard to be with her. Although he hadn't known it at the time, he'd realised over time that she'd been just as unhappy as he was. Anytime they fought, she would always talk about leaving him and starting over a long way away, but stuck it out for as long as she could and he assumed she did so because of their daughter, Zoe.

My little sweetheart.

He wished he could have been there for her more, but with his marriage to Molly growing more distant by the day, a void had been created. A gap that he could never bridge – especially after the day Molly vanished into thin air.

It had been a typical summer's day. Zoe was out playing with her friends, doing things that ten-year-olds do during the holidays. Adrian sat in the garden, sunning his expanding belly, beer in hand. He could recall every word Molly had said that day – none of which was out of the ordinary, except for some strange ramblings about *travelling across the stars*; but considering she was a bit of an astrology buff, he'd figured she was just spouting some zodiac nonsense. Normally when he mocked such a thing, she'd get upset and sometimes fight with him, but not on that particular day. No, on the day she went missing, she just up and left the house. An act of randomness. A bolt out of the blue. No bags or anything that suggested she was leaving for a long time. And at the time, he'd figured she'd had enough of his bullshit, fallen into what seemed like a trance and left. If that was the case, she'd have been back in a few hours, ready to start the bickering all over again. But not that day. Molly vanished and left her family with a lot of unanswered questions.

Seven years gone. And today was the anniversary – which plagued Adrian. He could sense the weight of the date all week and drank to mask the grief, especially after the Ryan family solicitor called and reminded him that in Ireland, after seven years, a missing person is officially declared dead – which he was well aware of. A funeral had already been organised to help give Molly's parents some closure.

A smell of diesel filled his nostrils while he stroked his long beard. Dark thoughts crossed his mind and he did not have a shred of guilt for drinking on the job. He didn't care for the safety of his passengers or what his boss thought of him. In fact, accelerating the engine was one of the only aspects in his life where he still felt totally in control.

Adrian wished he was heading for destination unknown and not some commuter town on the outskirts of Dublin – which was now rapidly falling into a state of decay due to political upheaval. He figured it would not be long before it was in a complete state of dystopia, and its downfall over the last year or so had contributed significantly to his family's financial issues.

What hope does my beautiful Zoe have in this world of ruthlessness? Fuckin' elite classes hoarding money and wealth while the rest of us starve outside their gated communities.

He didn't care as the alcohol slid effortlessly down his throat; the sensation of his first drink of the day was enough to help him black out the smell of his train. Diesel fumes, oil, machinery and old industry, his senses were assaulted by it all on a daily basis. Still though, he enjoyed his work. It gave him a chance to clear his head and the last journey of the night was his favourite. Just him and the dark tracks, in solitude.

Some of the stations were lit up well, but the further he got away from the city, the less the stops looked like actual train stations. More of a baron platform, with a single sign, the perfect spot for a potential victim of crime to find themselves.

After leaving his penultimate stop, he couldn't help but notice that an unusual amount of people had gotten off for this time of night, leaving the carriages lifeless and hollow. With another chug from the beer bottle, he pushed hard on the accelerator. The engine roared into life and gathered speed quickly. *Only ten minutes to go, may as well see what this baby can do.* He turned the radio on, tuned to his favourite station and cranked the volume. The sound of Axl Rose screamed around the cabin.

As the train passed under a bridge, static cut into the tune, pulling him from his private party, and that's when he realised that he was pretty drunk. He checked himself in the side mirror, his eyes red and tired. He didn't feel as fatigued as he looked, so shrugged it off with a laugh and went back to tuning the radio. Within the static, he heard a woman's voice saying his name. Then he heard it again, only this time more clearly, and even though he hadn't heard her speak in seven years, he was sure it was Molly.

For fuck's sake, Adrian, get yourself together, man!

He slapped himself, figuring it was just his mind playing tricks on him. Surely a declaration of death and her anniversary would do that to a tired old drunk?

Adrian could not see more than four or five feet ahead as the train swallowed the tracks. He laughed, thinking about how a fox or deer wouldn't stand a chance if they got stuck in the headlights. And that was when it happened. It only took a second, but that second seemed to last forever... a woman was on the tracks, staring into the cabin, eyes locked to his. Her mouth was open, but whatever sound she made could not be heard over the static which now boomed from the speaker. And then there was nothing. Silence in the cabin.

At first, Adrian thought he was dreaming. He noticed his pale face in the side mirror and the hairs on his arms and neck stood on end, his skin prickled. Then reality hit him hard as the blood splattered across the window came into focus.

What the fuck?

Those three words repeating again and again in his mind, with the occasional outburst. "What the fuck!?" He could not think straight, panic set in, and although he wanted to stop the train, he couldn't. Something within compelled him to keep going.

When the train came to a stop at the final station, he took a step back away from the controls and watched his hands as they relentlessly shook.

"What have I done? Why did I have to speed?"

He exited the cabin and walked round to the front of the train, expecting to see some poor soul mashed across it. He was relieved to find nothing more than a few streaks of blood. Was the train going so fast that the body liquidised, like a fly hitting a car windscreen when driving on the motorway during summer? Without thinking, his body started to move and before he knew what was happening he had gotten some old oily rags from a compartment in the cabin and begun cleaning the blood from the glass.

"Hey, pal. What'd you hit?" A familiar voice spoke from behind him, gravelly and old. He knew it belonged to James Mulligan – a security guard who worked the late shift at the station.

Adrian spun round and locked eyes with him. "Oh, hey Jim, err… nothing major. A deer, I think?"

"Ouch, damn thing must have taken the head off, eh?"

Adrian exhaled a nervous laugh. "Yeah, maybe."

"Where did this happen?" Mulligan asked, seemingly intrigued by the situation.

"Ah, it happened about a half hour ago," Adrian lied. "I was only about two or three stops outside of the city." It was at this point Adrian realised that he'd been drinking. "But, you know, it's getting late and I want to get home. Zoe will be waiting up for me."

"I hear you, pal. I was going to ask if you wanted to come for a quick pint? My shift is just about finished now that you've pulled in. Time for lights out and lockup."

"Maybe some other time, Jim. As I said, my kid—"

"Are you alright? You're looking a bit pale…"

Adrian didn't have time for chit chat and opted to end the conversation as quickly as he could. He needed to get out of here. With no body plastered to the train, it was quite possible that some poor soul was lying beside the tracks somewhere in need of help. "I'm fine, Jim. Look, I have to go."

"No problem, pal. Go home and get some sleep. You look like you need it. And hey, don't feel guilt over the deer, pal... happens all the time." Mulligan laughed.

Adrian didn't.

"Pints next time, yeah?"

"Sure," Adrian replied, before stuffing the oily rags into his backpack, slinging it over his shoulder and making his way to the carpark. He glanced back to see Mulligan watching him as he went, which didn't help his sense of paranoia.

In the car, he slapped the steering wheel in frustration. "Fuck!" His hands were still shaking. He took a few moments to compose himself and try and clear his thoughts. But the image of the woman's eyes kept flashing before him. Even when he closed his eyes, he could see them. It hadn't been long enough for him to register anything about the woman. He couldn't tell if he knew her. He couldn't even be sure what colour her hair was and didn't want to admit to himself that she resembled his missing wife. But the one thing he was certain of was that her eyes looked totally at peace, despite her gaping mouth. Whoever she was...

Fuck.

What if she wasn't dead? Did she try to leap out of the way at the last minute and was only partially caught by the speeding machine? Could she be lying on the side of the tracks gasping her last breaths? He supposed nothing would survive being hit at that speed and began formulating a plan. He recited it repeatedly to himself until he was convinced that this was the best course of action. After all, he had been drinking. If a body was found – dead or alive – this incident would be investigated and he could be in a world of trouble.

I have to find the body.

The roads were empty late at night, so he figured he'd stick to the back roads in the hope of avoiding a police checkpoint – to be breathalysed now would be a disaster. He thought ahead to when he'd arrive at the station. *Grab yourself a coffee from the petrol station on the way. That should help cover up the booze.* Everything had gone to plan so far, he'd got a double expresso and a bottle of water into him and even managed to stop his hands from shaking before he reached the station, thankfully without any brushes with the law. While parked outside, he took a moment to look at a picture of Zoe on his phone. *I'm sorry for drinking on the job, sweetheart. I have to go find out if I hit someone or not. Your daddy is no good to you in prison.*

He pocketed his phone, exited the car and made his way around back. In the boot, he rustled around and found his torch – one he'd bought in the event of changing a tyre at night. Never in a million years had he thought he'd be using it while searching for a body that he hit while driving a battering ram under the influence.

He trod carefully along the tracks, keeping a sharp eye open for whatever his torch exposed. It was quiet, almost eerie. The night sky was covered with dull clouds. Light pollution from the city could be seen in the distance, and the cold suddenly gripped him. With a shake of the head, he forced himself forward.

After about twenty minutes, he came to the spot where he guessed the incident had happened. But there was nothing to see other than train tracks, stones and grassy banks either side. The air was musty and foul, which started to give him a headache; well, it was either that or the booze wearing off and a hangover was creeping in. Even though he had run the train along the tracks for years, he struggled to get a sense of familiarity. And it was at this point his senses kicked in, a moment of absolute clarity, forcing an outburst. "What the fuck am I doing?"

He slumped to his knees and looked to some stars shining through a break in the cloud, hoping that he'd wake up at any moment, but he wasn't asleep. He was alive and in deep trouble if he couldn't find out whether he'd hit someone or not. A star shot across the sky, distracting him, and he realised he was completely alone. A depressing thought. Then the star vanished behind a dark piece of sky – not the night, but something, colourless, hovering between clouds. He stared at it for some time, trying to make sense of it, but whatever it was slowly faded from view, leaving him feeling exhausted and in desperate need of some rest.

I'm losing the plot. Hearing her on the radio, seeing her on the tracks and now some black egg in the sky?

He decided it was time to head home; to sleep and wash the day away. It was nearly 2 a.m. and he was surprised Zoe hadn't called him, wondering where he was. Perhaps she'd dozed off early, which would probably be for the best.

He didn't mind the long walk back to the car. Cold air helped clear his head and he figured if anyone came to question him over the woman or the blood on the train, he would claim he'd hit some local wildlife – that seemed like the best story to stick to. It wouldn't be the first time a train took out an animal, according to Jim Mulligan. And after all, what choice did he have?

Adrian's car was the only car in the carpark, and by the time he returned, a layer of frost covered the windows. He grabbed an ice-scraper from the boot and proceeded to cut away the chunks of ice. His hands were freezing and started to go numb. And that's when his phone rang.

Shit.

Adrian struggled to remove the phone from his pocket, almost dropping it as he did so, his cold fingers lacking the strength to grip the device. The screen flashed; the device vibrating in his hand. It took him a few seconds to realise that it was Zoe calling. He glanced at the time again, and a sense of worry shot through his body. He stabbed at the screen to answer before the call bounced to voicemail and with a quivering voice, he croaked, "Hello?"

"Dad, where are you?"

Adrian hesitated to answer her question. He had been gearing himself up all night to answer questions from the law, not from his daughter at 2 a.m. and for some reason he couldn't explain, he felt the need to lie to her. "I'm just leaving Jim Mulligan's house, sweetheart." He immediately regretted it as he anticipated her next question to be to ask why he was at a work colleague's house so late. But that question never came. Instead, there was a long pause. "Sweetheart? Are you there?"

"Dad," Zoe began, her voice laced with sorrow, "you need to come home."

"What's happened? Is everything okay, darling? You sound upset!"

"You need to come home now, please. I don't know what to do."

"I was heading home anyway, but is everything okay? You have me worried!"

Zoe paused again, and he could hear she was crying.

"No... It's Mam."

"What about your mother?"

Zoe broke down into tears and struggled to get the words out. And through the inaudible blubbers, Adrian just about made out Zoe's plea for him to hurry.

"I'm on my way."

For the entire journey home, a million thoughts raced through his mind. *What has happened at home? What could possibly have Zoe so upset?*

When Adrian pulled into the driveway, he leaped from the car and stormed into the house. In the living room he found Zoe on the couch – judging by the makeup all over her face, she had cried herself to sleep. He didn't wake her, but went to fetch a drink before doing anything. He needed something to help with the nerves, there'd been too much action for one day.

He made his way into the kitchen and grabbed hold of the fridge door and that was when something caught his eye; the same thing that must have caught Zoe's attention before she called him and plunged into tears. A piece of paper torn from an A4 pad with messy handwriting scrawled across it, addressed to him, dated seven years ago, signed by Molly.

His lips moved as he read, realising that his wife was really unhappy in their marriage and with her life. More so than him. In the first paragraph, she touched on the good times when they first got together. Carefree early days around the time when Zoe came into the world. Nevertheless, the letter quickly descended into the dark. She explained her struggles with depression and how she wanted nothing more than escape from her life. As hard as that was to accept, it still wasn't the heavy load that was about to land at his door. In the last paragraph,

Molly told him directly what she was going to do, as soon as she'd delivered this message. She would get up, leave the house and would probably never see any of them again. And that's when he realised the letter was written in Zoe's handwriting…

Adrian rushed to the living room, turned on the light and gently woke her.

"Dad?"

"Hi, sweetheart."

"What time is it?"

"Late."

She stirred, slowly adjusting her eyes, "Are you only just home?"

"Doesn't matter," he said, presenting her with the letter. "What's this all about?"

Zoe examined it and gave him a stern look. "You wouldn't believe me if I told you."

"Try me."

"No, you'll think I'm crazy."

"Sweetheart, I know today is a hard day, being her anniversary and all–"

"Yeah, and? It's not like you give a shit."

"Of course, I do. I loved your mother very much."

Zoe turned over towards the back of the couch. "That's not what she told me…"

Adrian rubbed his temples in frustration. "What?"

"I said you wouldn't believe me."

"Believe what? What happened?"

"She fucking spoke to me, Dad."

Adrian stood up and took a step back. "What?"

"Yeah, tonight. I was in the kitchen listening to the radio and I heard her. She was talking to me. Through the static! I wrote some of it down…"

"Sweetheart, please, you're just emotional—"

Zoe snapped round. "Don't you dare talk down to me. It happened. I'm not crazy or emotional. She contacted me, told me those things and I have to go find her."

Adrian couldn't believe what he was hearing. This was all some crazy dream, surely? It was the emotion of the anniversary. "Sweetheart, we bury her tomorrow…"

"We're burying an empty box, Dad!"

"Our family needs closure, darling. It's been seven years. No trace, nothing. We have to accept that she is gone and it is time to move on."

Zoe jumped up from the couch and stormed towards the door. "You believe whatever you want to believe, Dad. Whatever helps you sleep at night… I know she is out there somewhere and I'm going to find her."

Adrian watched her leave the room and listened to the heavy footsteps make their way upstairs. His head spun, so he plonked down on the couch and drank his beer. His thoughts raced and flooded with questions. *She killed herself seven years ago, I know she did. But what if she didn't? Is she haunting me? Haunting us? What is going on here? Are we all losing our minds?*

With his eyelids getting heavy, Adrian hadn't the energy to get himself up to bed – the thoughts of the funeral tomorrow were too much to process right now. Instead, he lay down his weary head and passed out.

Grief's infernal flower was in full bloom under the melancholy sound of the wind. Within a dream-like haze he watched a figure in black stand on the opposite side of the cold graveyard, eyes cloaked in darkness, taunting him from beneath the hooded shadow. Adrian could not take his eyes off it as it haunted the vicinity. *I really am starting to fucking see things...*

He followed the priest and watched intently as his wife's wooden coffin was positioned above the hole. Flowers with torn stems tapped gently against the lid as it descended deeper into the cold, dark earth. They say, when you die, a loved one or guardian angel comes to greet you and help shepherd you over to the other side, but as he watched the coffin hit the dirt, his focus shifted to the dark presence that wandered close by.

Adrian's appearance was scruffy, generally. Fond of a drink and not much else, but at least, for this day, he'd made an effort. Dressed in a sharp black suit with matching shirt and tie, he certainly looked the part of a grieving widower, although his face hung with an unwavering look of dread, eyes sunk inward filled with watery hopelessness. That said, he was doing a better job at keeping it together than Zoe had anticipated, which he supposed was the least he could do for his dearly departed.

Rumours circled suggesting Molly's suicide and for whatever reason nobody seemed to blame Adrian. In fact, the priest sympathised and figured he must have been in a lot of pain. Both sides of the family were in attendance, all feeling the awkwardness that is associated with death, but they still managed to emerge from their comfort zone and walk up to look both Adrian and Zoe in the eye and offer their sincerest condolences. After a while, Adrian found himself standing by the grave alone, staring into the abyss.

The gloomy menace continued haunting in the background and with every deep breath Adrian took, his eyes focussed past the priest and fixated on the shadow. It glided effortlessly with the grace and elegance of an Olympic rhythmic dancer. With every slide he watched the human-shaped cloud meander about.

Despite everything, Adrian knew it was all in his mind. He was not religious in any way, but he knew enough to know that good spirits don't come to welcome the souls of those who choose to exit the world. His family always thought that he'd be the one to make *that* selfish choice someday. After all, he was a drunk and on the road to ruin – or at least he was in the stereotypical sense of the word.

He looked at his daughter, who seemed to be holding it all together quite well. She'd never leave home without her customary black eyeliner, black vest, black jeans, black boots – in fact, everything in her wardrobe was black. He knew her peers slapped a goth label on her, which if you were to look at her and make a snap judgement could be true, but he always felt that beneath the dyed black hair, pale face makeup and dark clothing, she was just an artistic soul without a mother who needed to find her own way in this world.

The rain didn't let up all afternoon. It had accompanied the coffin and the hearse from the church to the burial ground. There had been frost on the ground that morning, but thankfully the grave had been dug the day before.

The winter-spring crossover brought a renewed sense of freshness to the land. Daffodils would bloom soon and some of the bare trees surrounding the graveyard began to bud. The air wasn't filled with pollen yet, but the smell was one that could be enjoyed, despite the heavens being open all afternoon.

Dirt hit the wood with a muffled thud in the rain. Someone in the nearby crowd cried while a woman, probably a neighbour, struggled to control a bout of dry coughing. And despite everything that was happening, Adrian found himself not lingering on guilt or the shadow that haunted the far side of the plot. Drifting in and out of coherence, the priest's raspy voice rising high and low had barely registered with him. In fact, the only thing that did register with him was the dancing shadow that continued to plague his vision. He couldn't help but feel he was struggling to deal with everything and as the cemetery emptied, mourners were met with strong gusts of wind and sporadic pelts of heavy rain – the type of rain that stung and could turn skin raw. Umbrellas didn't stand a chance and offered no shelter from the conditions.

He needed a drink.

At home, Adrian stood by the bath, watching steam rise and condensation build up on the white tiles. He needed to wash away the day and find some solace in the situation. But his thoughts were consumed with frightening images of his wife haunting him. If she was, then why? Was she trying to tell him something? A harbinger of brighter days? Or perhaps impending doom. He needed closure and the burial wasn't enough.

Hot water turned his skin red as he slid into the bath. He felt dizzy from the heat and took some time to relax. Then he lifted his arm from the water, over the side, reached down and grabbed a bottle of whiskey and proceeded to neck it straight from the bottle. After a while, he felt the effects and couldn't shake the thoughts of losing his mind over his missing wife. For seven long years he refused to believe she was dead. *No body, no death.* She had to be out there somewhere and the never knowing was becoming a cross too heavy to bear...

He reached down the side of the bath again, only this time he carefully picked up something smaller, shiny and sharp. He then lay his arm out along the top of the water, studying his veins, before allowing it to sink slightly below the surface. With the blade, he pressed hard and flickers of red danced along the steel.

This is it now, one final hard drag and I'll be free.

He tightened his grip on the blade and readied himself to pull it along his veins with a deep breath—

There was a loud bang, and Adrian dropped the blade. The bathroom door bounced off the doorstop and to his surprise, he saw Zoe standing there with a look of shock on her face.

"Dad?"

He didn't reply, instead he scrambled around in the water and tried to retrieve the blade.

"Dad!" Zoe screamed, finally realising what was taking place.

"Get out of here."

Zoe ran to him, reached in and grabbed both wrists. "What did you do!?"

"Stop, please—"

Zoe ignored his pleas and pulled his arms from the water; blood oozed beneath her fingers.

He went limp in her grip and before he knew it, floods of tears ran down his face. "I'm sorry, sweetheart."

She pitied him and they embraced.

Later that night, they both sat at the kitchen table without saying a word. Adrian knew what she was thinking, he could see it on her face. Confusion, despair and anxiety, all rolled into one big cluster bomb, waiting to go off. He felt guilt for what he'd done. "I'm sorry."

"No, you're not."

"I am, sweetheart. I just—"

"I don't want to hear it. First we lost her and your answer is to check out too?"

"I'm sorry, I wasn't gonna do it."

"Lies. If I hadn't found you, you'd be dead by now," Zoe shouted, bursting into tears.

"Maybe you're right, sweetheart. I'm losing it. I'm seeing her everywhere."

"What do you mean?"

"I've a confession. The night you heard your mother in the static... I heard her too."

"What? Why didn't you tell me?"

"I figured it was the occasion, or the booze, getting to me and my mind wasn't with it," he replied, then dropped his face into his hands.

"And you let me carry on thinking I was crazy?"

"I don't know what is going on, Zoe. Maybe she is haunting us or trying to send us a message?"

Zoe sat in silence, processing everything, then got up from the table and went to the shelf where he kept his booze.

"What are you doing?" Adrian asked.

"Something I should have done years ago..." she replied and then proceeded to uncap and pour his liquor down the drain.

He wanted to stop her, but something compelled him to say nothing and let her do her thing. After all, he did give her a serious scare and she was in just as much pain as he was, if not more.

When Zoe finished, she turned and stared at him. "Consider this an intervention, Dad. No more alcohol for you. It's time we accepted that she is dead and we are moving on with our lives."

Adrian was shocked by her sudden calmness and at how grown up she instantly sounded.

"Here's what is going to happen. I'm going to go stay with a friend of mine for a couple of days and you're going to get your shit together. Take a few days off work and put everything up to this point behind you, okay? Leave it in the past, Dad. Or else we won't have a future."

He understood her demands and did not argue. She was right. Whatever visions or sounds he was experiencing didn't matter anymore. It was time to put them all in the past, for her sake. She needed a father and he needed to be there for his daughter.

After Zoe packed a bag and left, barely saying goodbye, he felt alone in the empty house. He wanted to drink, but resisted the urge to go and get some booze. He figured the loneliness he felt now must have been what Zoe felt for the last seven years. A father there in body, but not in mind and like Molly, he was gone too.

She's dead and nothing I can do can ever bring her back. I don't know why she left us, but I think I understand now. Unhappiness drove her away and I hope wherever she is, she is at peace. I love you, Molly.

One week later, Adrian was feeling better, his thoughts no longer riddled with grief and the unknown. He hadn't felt the urge for drink since Zoe had intervened; a new routine had been established. He was up early, clean, exercising and eating well. His mood felt better and he'd already noticed a difference in his body. And with his new positive outlook on life, it was time to return to work and start getting everything back on track again.

Work was good for him. He enjoyed it and when asked to cover a week of late shifts, he was happy to accept. Loneliness no longer got to him. In fact, for the first time in as long as he could remember, he felt satisfied with everything.

He pulled into the carpark and readied himself to take the last train home. Outside, a soft layer of snow blanketed everything. The air was crisp and fresh and there wasn't a sound to be heard, other than the snow crunching underfoot as he made his way to the train.

On the platform, no passengers were waiting to board and that was okay with him. He noticed the sky had cleared and figured it'd be a peaceful journey.

"How ye, pal? Haven't seen you around in a while, you're looking better these days," a familiar voice said from behind.

Adrian turned to see James Mulligan standing by a ticket machine and smiled.

"Hey Jim, thanks."

"How about that drink later?"

"Sure thing, Jim," Adrian lied, and instantly wondered why. Perhaps he wasn't ready to tell people he was off the drink, statements like that are usually met with a series of questions. "Will call you in about an hour or so."

Mulligan didn't reply, instead he nodded with some sort of semi-salute, which Adrian took as an 'okay.'

After the engine roared to life, Adrian stuck his head out the window and shouted, "I hope there's no wildlife getting in the way tonight."

Laughing, Mulligan replied, "Just keep your eyes peeled, pal. Who knows what is out there at this time of night?"

The train rumbled along the tracks and Adrian watched the sky clear, revealing twinkling stars. On either side, snow covered the embankments and the track shined from the low temperature. He felt at peace from the ambiance of it all. He checked the cameras. There were no passengers tonight, they'd probably all taken a snow day from work and stayed home with their families, something he suddenly found himself wishing he could do.

Zoe... I wonder where you are now, sweetheart.

He knew she needed time to heal and hadn't chased after her. To press her after all she'd been through would only make matters worse. *An old head on young shoulders.* He knew she could take care of herself; she'd been doing so for the last seven years. Still, he couldn't help but wonder if she was okay and he promised to himself that he would be ready for her return.

Static crackled from the speakers, then sounds from his favourite radio station came through. He smiled and the train ran onward.

In the dark of the night, a sudden realization dawned on him... he was approaching the spot where he thought he had hit that woman. Her face flashed in front of him, an unwanted image at this time. He shook the thought from his head and tried to focus on the tracks; then his thoughts were interrupted by a hissing from the speakers. That familiar sound he knew all too well. "It's happening again!" he screamed.

His eyes searched the tracks, but there was nothing. With panic, he turned the radio off, but the static still crackled and hummed. Sweat began running down his back and he felt himself slipping. Then his reactions kicked in and he pulled the emergency brake lever that hung from the cabin ceiling. Beneath him, the wheels locked and began screeching on the tracks. Among the static he was sure he could hear Molly and Zoe calling to him. Was he losing his mind? Was this actually happening?

He expected to see the woman or even wildlife this time, but nothing appeared in front of the train. He feared the worst. Eventually, the train came to a halt and the static stopped. He could have sworn he heard Molly whisper to him.

He checked himself in the side mirror. His face was pale, his hands shook uncontrollably and that was when he realised he was in a state of shock.

We're here...

The words whispered to him again and the sounds from the speaker stopped.

Adrian exited the train and walked in front of it, his cold breath catching in the headlights. "Hello?" he shouted into the night sky. "Is there anybody out there?"

Silence.

"I'm losing my mind," he told himself over and over again. "Get yourself together, Adrian."

He took a moment to compose himself, deep cold breaths and a count of ten did the trick, for now. Exhaling, he searched the sky, his eye catching something that did not belong there. It was the black object he'd seen before, only this time there were no obstructions.

He walked down the tracks towards the thing. It hung in the sky, black and motionless, no light reflecting off it. Mesmerized and fixated on it, all sound seemed to vanish from around him. No crunch from the frozen stones between the tracks or air leaving his body. Time stood still.

Beneath the object, Adrian stared up, watching as it seemed to descend from the sky, slowly. As it got closer to him, he could hear a low droning.

"Hello?" he called out.

The object stopped about ten feet above him and the droning sound faded. He could see the thing was oval in shape and suddenly a small red light appeared at its centre. Deep down, he knew there was no reason to be afraid.

The light shone on him and with it he could hear static. Encrypted voices calling to him, telling him that everything would be okay now. And that was when he realised what was happening. Everything became clear. Molly had more to her than he could ever imagine. She'd spent years searching for help and was selected – summoned to the stars.

The object came closer and he noticed all the snow around him melt away, but could not feel any heat.

"I'm looking for my wife!" he shouted.

A bright spotlight replaced the red beam and surrounded him. He could no longer see anything that resembled earth., only white light and the black oval from which it came.

The static sound intensified and he could hear her, clearer now, the same words over and over again. *It's okay, honey, you have been selected. Let go of the past and come join us.*

"Molly? I don't know—"

Dad, it's okay. You have been selected. Come join us.

"Zoe? Is that you? What is happening?"

The static stopped, and he could feel himself starting to rise... and at first, he tried to resist by trying to drop to his knees, but there was no sense of gravity. Only light in all directions and the black oval within touching distance. Unable to blink, suspended in nothingness, he had no choice but to commit to the celestial power.

With the only remaining sense he had, he reached out and placed a hand on the oval. It was cool, like a stone. "Molly! Zoe! I'm here." And before he knew it, everything went dark and the sky was clear.

A cold breeze returned and the train stood idle, its task incomplete and with it, headlights began to fade, plunging the machine into darkness. Above, something streaked across the sky, its origin and destination unknown.

THE
OBSESSED

The thought of a blade running along her wrist made Garima Kapoor feel sick, but this didn't stop her from searching for that elusive feeling – a sensation that she found hard to explain when she tried to justify her actions to herself. And as the blood ran down her hand, dripping from her fingers, she thought to herself *I hate Mondays*. Or at least she thought it was Monday? It was hard to tell these days with insomnia corrupting her mind...

Beneath her eyes, black sacks hung, weary and tired. It was hard to focus on anything, resulting in her parking herself in front of her window watching the world go by – with a sugar-loaded coffee in one hand, and a blade in the other; an activity she didn't mind all that much. In fact, she found the road outside her house to be quite interesting. Her neighbours to the left – the Carroll family – were involved with some sort of political party. She'd often see them coming and going on their campaign trails – not to mention the number of random visitors that arrived. She couldn't know for sure, but imagined that they were a bit of a shady family.

The neighbours to the right – the Whyte family – were slightly odd, but outgoing and friendly. The father was a retired teacher of some sort and, judging by the number of empty bottles in the garden, his wife was heavy on the wine. Her family wouldn't normally mix with the Whytes; not until Christmas time rolled round – a time of year which the Kapoor family had to grin and bear for the sake of neighbourly civility.

Despite daydreaming and cooking up fantasies about her neighbours, Garima couldn't help but turn her attention to the bungalow directly across the road. Her parents – Sanjay and Danika Kapoor – often mocked her by calling her a *curtain twitcher!* And her father even bought her a set of binoculars as a joke present.

Her view went directly into the kitchen and in there she'd watch Henry Maguire pottering about. Sometimes with binoculars, sometimes without – it all depended on what mood she was in. Despite him being much older, he was her secret crush. One she would dream about when she did eventually drift in and out sleep.

Henry was different to the rest of the families on the road. He lived in solitude and didn't converse with his neighbours. No one knew his circumstances, nor his profession, so it didn't take long for some rumours to circulate about him. Some said he used to be in the army and never had the chance to marry. Others reckoned he was an artist – you know, one of those creative types that needed to be alone in order to work. Whatever the backstory, it didn't stop Garima thinking about him. Perhaps it was the mystery that attracted her to him. In her mind, he could be anything she wanted him to be. And this was her secret. One that lay deep inside of her.

Her desires would upset her parents, both of whom embraced their Indian heritage. This was something that Garima didn't care too much for. She had never been to India as she'd been born and raised in Ireland. But she had done her best to respect her parents. So, the thoughts she harboured for Henry had to stay behind closed doors.

He's too old for me anyway. It'd never work...

Still, she couldn't help but daydream. And that was the least of her parents' worries. While they focused on getting her through her studies and sleep deprivation, little by little, she experimented with razor blades against her wrists. In her mind, this was not a suicide attempt, but more of an unquenchable thirst – a need to feel.

Henry was a handsome man – in a rugged sort of way; his hair was grey and neat. His physical condition assisted with hiding his age as he walked around like a man in his twenties. Confident, strong, showing every characteristic an alpha male should possess. She hoped he was a doctor. Why this mattered, she couldn't understand. Perhaps it was years of her parents' conditioning and goal setting.

Rain fell hard against the path outside. Puddles swelled. Droplets teemed down the outside of her window, leaving a residue. Condensation slowly built up on the inside. Using her index finger, she wrote the words *I hate myself* in the mist.

As the drops dribbled down the window, her gaze reached beyond the moist haze into Henry's kitchen. There he stood, wearing his tartan pyjama bottoms and tight grey t-shirt. As he made his way across the room, she wondered if his bare feet were cold from the tiled floor. Unable to focus on her studies, she was able to study him. Watching his every move, she thought to herself, *maybe everything isn't so bad after all.*

Henry stood over the sink, preparing food for dinner. He washed vegetables beneath the tap and placed them on the draining board. Beside the sink, he set up a chopping board and pulled out a large knife and sharpening steel. With quick action, the edge returned to the knife.

As mundane viewing as it was, it didn't stop Garima staring as Henry chopped away at what looked like onions and that was when she gasped in shock...

She watched in horror as the knife slipped from his grip and in an instant, Henry was on the floor clutching his foot – his screams bellowing all over the estate. He backed away from the sink, across the room and into full view. Beside him a pool of blood rapidly grew. She watched him struggling to reach for a tea towel, eventually grabbing it, wrapping the cloth around his foot as tight as he could.

Garima looked on in shock at the poor man. All of her impulses urged her to seek help, but at the same time she was unable to look away. She reached for the gift her father gave her, which she kept stored on a shelf above her desk. Moving quickly, she fumbled the binoculars from the case, and with a quick toggle on the focus wheel, she was able to see Henry up close. The tea towel was soaked in dark red liquid. He sat motionless on the floor, pale-faced, with his back against the wall.

The urges to help in some way hadn't diminished, but she didn't want anyone to know that she was watching him – through binoculars, no less. Her father would be disgusted with her. But all of these thoughts left her mind as soon as she laid eyes on the little peach-coloured lump that edged the pool of blood.

Henry's big toe; severed, lifeless.

The mere sight of it caused her to wretch, violently. She scrambled around, grabbing hold of the waste paper basket beside her desk, as the contents of her stomach emptied in a violent wave of convulsions.

Henry, you fool. How did you manage to let it slip?

She wondered how long it'd take for the ambulance to get here. Or if he'd be too proud to call it, and would drive himself to the emergency room? Surely not. Not with that foot. She couldn't help but keep an eye on her watch as time crept by. All the while, Henry sat on the floor, holding the towel firm with one hand and inspecting his severed toe in the other. He seemed so calm about the situation – it was almost disturbing to watch.

She took a few moments to rub her eyes, and went back to check on Henry. He had moved and the floor had been cleaned. *But how?* It didn't matter because the man hobbled back into view with a frying pan in hand. He successfully struck a match and lit the burner on his oven. After the frying pan was set down, a splash of olive oil soaked the inside of the pan. *How could he continue cooking after what had happened?*

Garima was dumbfounded.

He really is strange... However, the strangeness quickly changed to horror when she noticed what Henry was preparing for his meal. At first, she refused to believe it, but there it was, sitting in the middle of the pan, simmering away – Henry's eyes were wide with excitement, almost euphoric.

She couldn't fully grasp what was happening and after a few minutes, Henry proceeded to plunge a fork into the toe and raise it up for a close inspection. With a quick lick of his lips and a dash of salt, he began to gnaw away at it – forcing Garima to reach for her bin, again.

"You sick, sick man," she repeated over and over again, as she wiped vomit from her mouth, reluctantly reaching for the binoculars again. This time, her hands shaking, she fearfully gazed through them, terrified of what she might see.

When her focus cleared, Henry stood in the window gazing up at her. With a scream, the binoculars hit the floor and she ducked for cover. *Shit, did he see me?*

A thump on the door forced her to recoil with fright. *He couldn't have made it over here that quickly. Could he?* She waited to hear who was at the door, chewing on her nails.

"Garima, darling? Are you okay?" Her mother called to her from the other side of the bedroom door. *Oh, thank fuck for that.*

"F-F-Fine, Mother. Just studying," Garima answered with a stutter.

"Well, okay. Dinner is almost ready. Come down when you're ready."

Dinner? Was she serious? The thought of food right now made her shiver. But, she was hungry. With a great effort, she managed to pull herself up from the floor and pulled on a jumper, making sure to cover her scabbed wrists before joining her family for   dinner.

Sanjay and Danika exchanged awkward looks across the table. They didn't have to say it out loud, but they knew something wasn't right with their daughter. She'd been this way for months and the lack of progress surrounding her insomnia had reached a frustrating point. Beneath the table,

Sanjay lightly kicked his wife, prompting her to try and open the lines of communication.

"How is the studying coming along, Garima?" Danika asked, clearing her throat.

"Fine, I guess," she replied, not looking up from her dinner plate.

"You haven't touched your food. Is there something wrong?"

Garima didn't answer.

"Your mother is talking to you, Garima," Sanjay said, firmly.

Garima didn't want to engage in conversation. Thoughts of the severed toe kept swirling around in her mind: *How could he eat it?*

"Garima... We're worried about you. You're not eating. You're not sleeping. Is there something else going on?" Her mother wasn't giving up; placing her hand on the table beside Garima in an attempt to show support.

"I said I'm fine. Look, I'm not in the mood to eat. May I just be excused?"

"No," Sanjay said, "your mother is talking to you. What is going on with you lately? All you do is sit up in your room looking out of the window."

"So, what's wrong with that?" Garima protested.

"Look at the bags under your eyes. They are pitch black. You need to stop stressing over your exams and go out and see your friends. You never see them anymore."

"That's rich, coming from you, Dad. You're the one who wants me to get perfect results, go to college and marry a doctor. An Indian one at that. You're the one forcing me to do things I don't want to do," Garima snapped.

"Oh, here we go again. I never said anything like that, Garima. I just want the best for you," Sanjay argued.

"Okay, stop! Can everyone just stop, please?" Danika exclaimed, forcing a silence at the kitchen table.

Garima looked around.

Both parents stared at her with their mouths open – clearly shocked by her outburst.

She knew they were both right, and they had every reason to be worried. Their only daughter looked unhealthy and lived like a recluse. It didn't help that outside of this, she obsessed over her neighbour – one who was roughly thirty years older than her – and this compounded her dark feelings. She hid the results beneath the baggy sleeve of her jumper. Concealing them was the easy part. As, too, was managing the rate at which she cut – but after witnessing Henry's actions tonight, she felt overcome with despair and sorrow.

She worried deeply for him.

Morning crashed into her room with the sun carrying a surprising amount of heat for the time of year, and by some miracle, Garima had managed to get a few hours' sleep.

In school, Tuesdays were the busiest with heavy lectures running all day. She normally left the house just after both parents went to work. The bus would arrive at half-eight, sharp. Feeling exhausted, she rose up from her bed, made her way over to the dresser and was shocked by the girl looking back at her in the mirror.

Her eyes, zombie-like, scared her. What had she become? Love wasn't supposed to do this to a person, was it? She slowly put some clothes on and fixed her long dark hair into a ponytail. The bus would be here in a few minutes and she didn't have the energy to rush. She moved to open the window to let some fresh air in.

The ground outside was dry, but the air seemed cold. She watched schoolchildren walking by with their bags on their backs, ready for class. She needed to get going, but was unable to find the motivation.

Henry's bungalow appeared idle – but his car was parked in the driveway.

Last night's events came rushing back into her mind. *He's still at home? Is he okay?* Her mind was made up. There would be no school today. How could she concentrate, knowing that he was at home and surely in need of urgent medical assistance for his foot. No, school would have to wait – Henry was important to her, even if he didn't know it, yet.

A cool breeze hung in the air as the morning crept on into the afternoon. And the road lay silent all day. She'd seen a cat scramble by earlier, but that was about the height of the excitement.

The curtains in Henry's kitchen had been drawn all morning, and she sat staring, gnawing at her nails, wondering if he was okay on the other side of them. *He's probably fine. Or he could be on the floor passed out from blood loss.*

Garima couldn't wait anymore. She battled with her inner thoughts, but in the end decided, it was time to go over and find out.

Garima walked across the road, moving with stealth-like precision. She felt silly, as she had walked up and down this road a million times. She paused to examine the gate as she approached it. It was a little rusty and she couldn't risk a sound that would signal to him that she was coming. Instead, she opted to climb over the front wall. If everything was okay inside the house, she'd need a reason to call over. And just dropping by in the middle of the day when she was supposed to be in school to check on a man who ate his own toe for dinner wasn't exactly the ice-breaker she wanted to use.

She crept up the garden to the house, making her way round to the side, positioning herself beneath the kitchen window – listening for sounds coming from inside.

Silence.

Her heart began to pound in her chest. She was so far outside of her comfort zone, it was almost exhilarating. The rush, oddly, was comparable to the sensation of running a razorblade down her arm.

Rising slowly to her feet, looking over the window ledge through the glass, the rush quickly diminished into disappointment when she saw that the curtains were still drawn.

A cold gust blew straight through her, putting her back on edge. She felt as if she was being watched. But she had to know if Henry was okay or not.

The kitchen was a corner room and the window faced towards the main road, but there was a wooden gate leading through to the back garden at the side of the house.

The side gate took a little bit of work to open, but was easy enough, which allowed her to creep into the back garden – her back tight against the bungalow's exterior wall. At the rear of the house was a large sliding door made of glass – she cautiously looked in.

Beyond the glass, she was relieved to find the curtains were pulled back. She searched for the pool of blood, but only saw minor stains from the night before.

Nothing seemed out of place.

Everything was tidy and clean; the kitchen table untouched, the worktop counters clear. The oven, however, still had the frying pan out on top of its hob. Standing upright now, she manoeuvred to get a better look. The pool of oil was still inside, but that was about it. *Why would he clean the kitchen and leave the unclean pan out?*

With a shake of the head Garima dashed nervously across to the other side of the patio door. From this angle, she could see the entire kitchen and beyond the oven, she laid eyes on him.

Henry, naked, knife in hand, stood with an almost hypnotic stare that led to nowhere.

At first, she jerked behind the wall to avoid being seen, but then she gasped at what was revealed in front of her.

The top half of his body was okay. Nothing out of the ordinary. She even made a note about how fit he was; however, it was the lower half of his body that caused her to recoil. Both legs were bleeding from large, gaping wounds in his thighs.

Cutting oneself took precision – if the act was supposed to be the hunt for sensation – but whatever she got out of the small cuts on her arms, it was nothing compared to the butchery unfolding before her eyes. Muscle and flesh akin to the size of a large T-bone steak was being carved slowly from his leg. *How could he do this without screaming?* She watched him continue to work away, eventually removing the lump from his body.

Clamping her hands over her mouth, fighting hard not to be sick, she could feel herself starting to lose control.

Henry – looking weary and weak – stood poking the sizzling lump of flesh in the pan with a masochistic smile etched across his face.

Garima had seen enough and ran for the gate at the side entrance, vomit escaping between her fingers. She carelessly bumped against a recycle bin – knocking it over with a loud crash.

She couldn't breathe, feeling like her heart was about to stop. *He's going to catch me!* With adrenaline kicking in, she burst through the wooden gate, running as fast as she could – the gate slamming shut behind her after rebounding off the side of the house. The bang stopped her momentarily and that was when she heard the patio door open.

Fuck, he's coming to investigate!

Despite the panic, she made it down the garden path, throwing herself over the wall, ducking behind it so not to be seen.

The gate opened with a violent thud, causing her to freeze with fear. She could hear him turning the recycling bin back upright. Holding her breath, she stayed as quiet as she could. The road was empty and quiet. His footsteps could be heard crunching down on the cold grass. *Oh no, he's coming this way.* She looked to her left and right, but there was nowhere to go. If she moved now, he'd see her and know that she saw him. Above her head, his hands slammed down on the top garden wall, his breathing heavy. If he looked down, the game was over.

Garima closed her eyes.

"Fucking cat," Henry snarled.

She opened her eyes, and saw the neighbour's tabby cat sauntering down the road.

"Get out of here!" Henry shouted at the animal – throwing an apple at it, missing the target, but it was enough for the feline to scamper off out of sight.

She could hear Henry making his way back across his garden, allowing her to take a quick glance over the wall. Wrapped in a dressing gown, she watched him limp through the side entrance, out of sight. Finally, she could exhale a sigh of relief. She waited for the sound of the patio door closing, then made a run for the safety of her house.

In her bedroom, she slammed the door shut and sank down to the floor, her back against the wood as she struggled to gather her thoughts. It was incomprehensible. *This was beyond insane. Why was he doing that to himself?* So many questions. And too many to process right now. She dashed across her room to close the blinds and noticed that the view into his kitchen was once again clear. She froze on the spot. Had he seen her run back into her house? Surely he wasn't quick enough to get back inside and draw back the curtains in time? No time to think. She yanked on the string, slamming the blinds shut, and fell to her knees hyperventilating.

There was a sombre mood at the dinner table. Garima's parents put it down to a bout of depression and lack of sleep. However, this didn't stop them from trying to extract whatever little bits of information they could from Garima, but she wasn't saying anything. How could she? What she had witnessed earlier in the day was almost too much to process, and it was plaguing her mind. Some things that are seen, can't be unseen. And the horror pinned itself to the forefront of her thoughts.

Later that night, alone in her bedroom, Garima sat silently in the dark. Despite everything, she still worried for him. What if he was just like her? What if he was only doing it so that he could *feel?* She understood that urge. That *need.* But whatever way his mind worked, he had crossed over to an extreme form of sensation seeking.

Looking at her scars, her mind cast back to why she opened her skin regularly. She rationalized it as a release of her fears, but unlike Henry, her cuts were allowed to heal. And that was the part Garima found herself struggling with.

Darkness engulfed the road. Neighbourhood cats scrambled about beneath the orange glow from the streetlights. Above this, a cold mist gently fell, kissing everything with a delicate moisture. A scene so pretty, it could be pasted across a postcard.

However, Garima's eyes could only focus on one thing – Henry's kitchen window.

She watched him as he stood in the window, gazing out across the road back at her. In her world, time stood still as their eyes locked. And she could not help feeling him staring straight through her, deep into her soul. While lost in his gaze, she didn't have to open her mouth and she knew he had seen her earlier today.

The passing moment seemed like eternity, and eventually, Henry made a slight signal to her. It took her a few seconds to decipher what he was trying to say. But then she understood. He was inviting her over.

Garima waited until her parents were in bed before sneaking out the back door, across the road, over to Henry's bungalow. The night air was cold against her face.

At the front door, she was fully alert to what was happening. Despite the obvious apprehension, her body kept moving as if it was stuck on autopilot. She took a deep breath, avoiding the doorbell, and tapped her knuckles gently against the door.

It opened with a slight creak, revealing Henry. He smiled and slowly pulled the door open, standing back and gesturing for her to enter.

The madness of it all. What did she really know about this man? Why was she risking so much?

Inside the house, she was not expecting to find it immaculate and pristine. Even in the hard to reach corners of the hall, not a ball of dust, nor a cobweb were to be found.

They made their way into the kitchen. Garima stood awkwardly as she watched Henry cover the knives on the countertop with a tea towel. She noticed that he wore a long brown dressing gown – covering his mutilated body.

Garima examined him, gasping at the void where his toe used to be.

"What have you done to yourself?" she asked.

Henry didn't reply. Instead, he went to the shelving above the fridge and pulled out a bottle of red wine, then made his way over to the table where two glasses were already waiting for him to pour. He gestured to her to take a seat and then poured some wine.

Garima reluctantly joined him. "I don't drink," she said softly as she slid into the chair.

"A little bit of alcohol is the least of our worries, don't you think?" Henry replied, before taking a large mouthful. The expression on his face suggested that his taste buds clearly tingled with enjoyment.

"I suppose," she answered, raising the glass to her nose. The smell was strong, fresh, alien to her. "Why do you do it?" she asked, while swallowing her first mouthful of wine. Her throat burned, and she started to cough.

Henry watched as she fought to control the coughing. After she composed herself, he took a sip from his glass. "You know why."

"What do you mean?" she asked.

"I've seen you. For months you've done things up in your room. Things that should be kept private. But you stood in front of open blinds," he answered, his tone firm and convincing.

"I only wanted to feel alive..."

"As did I. But cutting isn't enough. You've a bit to go before you realise that..."

Garima knew exactly what he was talking about. It started with a little bit of nail biting. Before long, all the nails on her hands were chewed to their stumps. It satisfied her at first, but soon, it wasn't enough. And from biting her nails down to raw bloody skin, she'd escalated to slight nicks from a blade. Light cutting soon followed, evolving into deep, scarring wounds. Never fatal, but close enough to experience the thrill of it all.

"I saw what you did last night," she stated.

Henry shrugged. "And? Isn't that the point of obsession? To push the boundaries to the point of destruction?"

"Is this the reason you live alone?" she asked.

Henry didn't answer. Instead he stood up from the table, positioned himself in the centre of the kitchen and dropped his dressing gown – revealing his body. He stood before her – a mutilated man. His legs and torso had been sliced down to the tendons, with his wounds still oozing. Chunks of flesh had been carved out, leaving barely enough to stand on. "I've reached my limit."

Garima recoiled in shock, gasping, then fought to keep from vomiting again. After a few minutes, she opted to drink the glass of wine in one go. Then she blurted out, "You need help, Henry."

"Yes, I do. But who in their right mind would view this as normal behaviour? People in the outside world will only want to lock me away in some sort of hospital."

"Hospitals are where people go to get help," Garima innocently claimed.

"What would you know about hospitals?" he snapped.

"Well, my parents want me to be a doctor someday."

"Ha, really? Tell me, doctor, what's the cure for someone whose only desire in the world is to consume himself?"

Garima paused for a moment, studying his eyes, watching for sincerity. And when she knew that he was a man in pain, she couldn't help but take pity on him. "You need someone who understands you."

Henry dropped to his knees, sobbing.

Garima went over, picked up his gown, and draped it over him. She gave his shoulder a reassuring squeeze and went to his kitchen cabinets. She dug out the first aid kit, then knelt down in front of the crying man. Without a word, she slowly tended to his legs.

She bandaged his limbs as best she could. He seemed thankful, but didn't express any emotion. She noticed him looking at the scarring on her arms, then he moved slowly and gently rubbed his finger along one of the bigger ones. "You understand. Don't you?"

"I think so…"

"Then you must give it a try."

Garima didn't answer. There was something in the way he spoke that she trusted. She felt his pain, and yet, suffered from it too. She watched him struggle to his feet and make his way over to the countertop. Henry Maguire, the man across the road. A man she'd secretly fancied for years, but now, she knew that she was looking at her soulmate. The one she was destined to be with. *Fuck the age gap. Fuck what my parents and friends would think. They would never understand what my beloved would bring into my life. An understanding of how our minds work. A balanced equilibrium. Yin and yang in perfect harmony.* She felt faint.

He held out the knife, handle first, offering it to her.

At first, she was hesitant, but allowed herself the time to shake any worries from her mind. She ran her fingers along the blade, lightly – the steel cool to the touch.

Henry studied her. "You understand, Garima. I suggest you begin where I began. Don't go too deep. And take it easy. I'm here and will guide you."

Using her free hand, Garima, unbuttoned her jeans and allowed them to slide down, revealing her thighs.

"Remember. Not too deep..."

She nodded and took the blade to the side of her leg. The incision was effortless. The escaping blood gave her a warm sensation. With sharp bursts, the knife silently carved its way down, blood oozing down her leg, staining her jeans. She didn't care. It was euphoric in the most unimaginable way. When she eventually had a chunk of flesh in her hand large enough, she tore it free, causing her to scream with joy.

"You did it. Well done!" Henry exclaimed.

Garima smiled and handed the lump of flesh to him. "I did it for you."

Garima felt ashamed of herself after finishing her meal. Not a whole lot of preparation had gone into the cooking – it was almost blú. However, she followed his instructions, sprinkled salt, and gnawed away at it until it was gone. She had transcended into unknown territory and wanted to burst into floods of tears – but she managed to keep the floodgates firmly closed.

"Where do we go from here?" she asked, nervously.

"We continue what I've started," Henry said with confidence, almost as if it was a matter of fact.

"And what is that exactly?"

"You're a smart girl, Garima. You know what. My work." He boasted – his mood shifting from down and out to upbeat and eager.

"Your work?"

Henry could sense the anxiety eating away at her, so he trod carefully with his words. He explained slowly that he had eaten human flesh before. The details of who were never disclosed, but he reassured her that he was not a murderer and it was a willing participant who shared the same desires.

"I know you've been watching me, Garima. I knew it from the first day that I moved onto this road. I left my windows open for you to see and you watched. I could sense that you needed me, but I had to show you, instead of telling you. You would have never understood otherwise."

Garima felt special.

All this time, he'd actually been calling to her. She was in pain and he was the only one offering understanding and guidance. She couldn't think of a response other than, "Thank you."

Henry nodded in acknowledgement. "Which brings me to my next request..."

"Anything."

"Our appetite is large and we're going to need some more soon..."

Garima didn't know or like where this was going. Eating her flesh had sickened her. She desired the cutting. Bleeding even. But, consumption was beyond her.

"Don't be coy. You had your first taste today. It'll take a while before you are comfortable with it. Trust me. And I promise you, you'll crave more soon. And it gets better every time."

Garima didn't reply. Instead, she stared down at the floor, but still hung on to his every word. Was he making sense? He seemed to be in total control and this was reassuring. But what would this life cost? "I don't want to kill anyone," she eventually said.

"It's part of my process. No, wait. I'm sorry, I meant, 'our' process," Henry stated, "I've been living this way for years. But with someone like you in my life, we don't have to live in the shadows anymore."

"Someone like me?"

"Yes! You understand the desire. You crave it. Together we can seek and rejoice in it," he said, almost hyperactive with excitement.

Garima nodded in agreement. "Okay. I'm in."

Outside the weather took a turn for the worse and heavy rain pelted against the windows. All night they extracted flesh from each other – dining in each other's flesh over candlelight.

The bad weather escalated into a storm. Thunder clapped, with flashes of lightning occasionally lighting up the candlelit room – it was the least of their concerns... until the flash revealed a figure standing in the patio doorway – Sanjay.

"Dad!" she shrieked, jumping up from the table. The action prompted a moment of chaos, with Garima grabbing the dressing gown off the floor to cover herself, while Henry backed away and stood over by the sink.

"Garima, let me in now!" her father roared through the glass. His rain-soaked face did nothing to hide the rage burning in his eyes.

Garima unlocked and opened the door, with her father barging his way into the kitchen. As he took in the bloody sight before his eyes, his expression shifted to a mix of rage and confusion.

"Dad, what are you doing here?" she asked, petrified.

"I saw you through your bedroom window. What the fuck are you doing here? What has he done to you? What is this?" her father shouted, turning his attention to Henry.

"Dad, wait. You don't understand. We're, err, friends," Garima tried...

"Friends? What are you talking about?"

Henry didn't like to feel cornered, let alone threatened. He grabbed hold of the large chopping knife on his worktop, and pointed it at the intruder, "Don't you dare come near me." he warned.

"I'm going to kill you for what you have done to my daughter. You sick fuck!"

"Dad, no!" Garima begged. She grabbed hold of her father's arm and tried to reason with him.

Henry looked on as Garima tried to restrain her father. "Let him go, Garima. I'm the one defending my home. If he comes near me, I will defend myself."

"Shut up, Henry. This is my dad."

"Henry?" Sanjay said looking at her with disbelief, "You're on a first name basis with this guy? Oh darling, you know nothing about him."

Henry straightened up at the impending accusation. He stood wielding the knife, and listened to Garima's father explain why he lived alone and why no one on the road would talk to him.

Sanjay explained that Henry had moved into town with a reputation. He'd committed some crimes in other parts of the country, so he and his wife moved onto their road. No one believed the rumours, and Garima was too young to remember, but after a while, Henry and his wife had become reclusive. Days turned to months and eventually it got to a point where the neighbours wondered where his wife was. Henry claimed she left him – ran off with some guy she fell in love with in the local pub. No one knew for sure, but the rumours about his past came flooding back and it didn't take long for them to be applied to this case. The local shops eventually stopped serving him and he became known as *The Wife Eater*.

"Don't believe a word, Garima," Henry protested. "It's all lies."

"Lies? How do you explain all of this then? You're a sick bastard!" her father shouted.

Garima tugged on her father's arm again, making him look at her. She begged him to go home, but before he could reply, Henry ran over and grabbed him from behind, holding the knife to his throat.

"Don't move," Henry ordered, his tone darkening, "Or I'll kill you."

"Henry, please, let go of him!" Garima cried, borderline hysterical.

"No. Think about it, Garima, my love. No one knows he is here. We could eat and even freeze some of him," Henry reasoned.

"That's my father you're talking about!" she shouted.

Sanjay struggled in Henry's grip, knowing the man was weak, but he couldn't take any chances with the blade so close to his throat. Instead, he tried to calm the situation. "Darling, it is okay. Everything is going to be okay."

"It sure is, neighbour," Henry whispered into his ear.

"Henry, please don't do this. I thought you cared about me!" Garima begged.

"I do. I'm doing this for us. We can give into our deepest desires. We need to seize the opportunity."

Garima broke down into tears. "Please not my dad. Anyone but him."

"The consumption of those we love, satisfies the most."

The statement struck a chord inside Garima. *He did it! The sick fucker murdered and ate his wife. If I join him now, he'll make me eat my father. Then how long would I have to wait before he turns on me like he did with his wife?*

"Okay, Henry. You're right. But, I need to be the one who finishes him. He is one I love and it's my choice to make," Garima pleaded.

Henry forced her father onto his knees, still keeping the blade pressed against the man's throat. A dark silence descended. Thunder continued to roll outside and another flash of lightning lit up the room.

Henry slowly took the knife away from her father's throat, then offered it to her. "The consumption of those we love, satisfies the most..."

Garima repeated the statement and reached out to take the blade from him. Her hands shook violently as her fingers slowly wrapped around the handle. As soon as she was in full control of the blade, Henry backed away from the situation and began singing softly.

Garima looked her father deep in the eyes. It was the first time she had ever seen him afraid. He knelt in fear of his own flesh and blood. "I'm sorry, Father," she whispered.

"Darling, no."

"I'm sorry for everything!" she screamed, and in the same moment, she exploded forward, pushing past her father, knocking him to the floor, driving the blade into Henry's chest.

Henry stood back, gasping. Looking down, he could see the handle stick out of him. And although he couldn't see it, he felt the steel inside him, slowly taking away his ability to breathe.

"Gar, Gaaar... Garima. How could—?" he stuttered, coughing, unable to finish his words before dropping to his knees.

Her father rose to his feet, placing his arms around his daughter. She was cold to the touch, but he could not break the gaze she had on Henry.

Garima watched him fade out.

A cold silence returned to the room. The storm outside was barely audible as both father and daughter were overwhelmed with the shock. She eventually took her father's hand, turned to him and said softly, "I want to go home."

The dining room table harboured a sullen mood. Sanjay sat in silence looking at her – she was a shadow of her former self – in both mind and body.

Her mother made numerous attempts to get food into her, and also get her to speak, but all her efforts ended in futility.

Instead, Garima just stared at the candle that flickered in the middle of the table. She looked into the heart of the flame, taking the time to think about every emotion that swirled around in her body. Love. Loss. Suffering. Desire. All equally dominating, but all had their beautiful moment.

"Darling, please eat something," her mother implored. "It's your favourite. Lamb. A little rare, the way you like it."

Garima shot her a look. If only her mother knew the full extent of the horrific events across the road. A horror that was now nothing more than local lore, probably soon to be myth. What the neighbours thought, they'd never really know. Perhaps Henry Maguire took off and re-joined his wife in parts unknown? Without a body, it was simply a missing persons case. With her eyes widening, Garima looked her mother in the eyes and sarcastically said, "No thanks, mother. I think I'm a vegetarian now."

Her mother's jaw dropped at the statement.

Garima looked up at her father. With a smile, she said softly, "The consumption of those we love, satisfies the most. Isn't that right, Dad?"

He didn't acknowledge her as he struggled to swallow his food.

"After appeasing that taste, nothing else will compare, Mother. Now let us all enjoy our sacred meal."

# FALL TO ZERO

As I walk across damp gravel, leaves begin to fall from trees. The sweet smell of Autumn is in the air. At the end of the road, two old round towers soar to the heavens, overlooking the village. It is a long climb to the top. My heart beats faster than it has in a long time; each step upward forcing exhausted breaths from my body. At the top, through the narrow window, I see fields surrounding the place I call home. Somewhere in the distance, farm machinery rumbles in harvest, droning as they seek to complete their task before the dark of winter. Unseen and below, birds sing and I think to myself, *What a beautiful day.*

I've been to the top of the towers many times, the view never failing to wow me. My eyes take it all in; lush green grass and crops stretching to the horizon. Below the great old towers, a modern village bustles with life and energy and a vibrancy that brings a smile to my face; cyclists, dog walkers, joggers and cars filled with parents and children on their way home from school, while the express bus brings those who commute to the city back safely.

The sky is clear at this time of day, which is why I like coming up here at lunchtime. Working from home feels like a prison sometimes, so I make it my business to absorb the splendour. I love it when there is a pale blue sky with little cloud to spoil the scenery. As I blow hot breath over my fingers, I wonder if everywhere is feeling the cold like I am now.

Somewhere below, a barking dog catches my attention. I can see it. In an idyllic playground, the animal is playing with some children, all of whom are laughing without a care in the world as they play on swings, slides, and a jungle gym. Some girls play skip-rope. Their sing-song weaves through the random burbling laughter of the kids. One of the young mothers walks behind her two-year-old son holding his hands up, while the others sit close by keeping an eye on their little darlings.

Sometimes I suffer from anxiety, but nothing like the wave that suddenly washes over me now. For no apparent reason, immense dread and despair cripples my very existence. Shaking my head to rid myself of these thoughts, I cannot keep the tears at bay. Emotions begin getting the better of me and I can feel it in my gut, something is happening beyond the horizon that I am yet to comprehend. I can't see nor smell it, but I know it is there. And *it* is happening.

I scream at the top of my lungs; imploring the village to listen, but no words surface. My cries are incoherent, unheard and pointless. My tear-soaked eyes search for the sun, hanging low in the sky, still shining bright on the poor souls below. I can see one of the mothers looking up at me and despite the great distance between us, I can sense and see fear etched across her face. She doesn't have to hear me to know *it* is on the way. I slap the stone wall with everything I've got; anything to warn her and the others to run. *It* is coming, I can feel it, but she turns away.

Moments before *it* happens, like a rush of air escaping a preheated oven, an intense heat invades my skin. I can smell burning, not sure from where. With haste, I quickly remove my winter coat, but it doesn't matter. *It* is happening and nothing I can do can stop it.

Beside the sun, a bright white light appears; an explosion in the sky, blinding my eyes, forcing me to cover my face in terror. Then I make myself watch the rising horror. Below it, a dull grey cloud descends to the Earth, reminding me of a mushroom-shaped tornado. Only instead of whirling winds, dry heat intensifies – turning my skin red, then black, blisters lifting and popping. I can feel the back of my throat burning and raw; unable to make a sound, I try to scream anyway.

The dog has stopped barking. The kids have stopped playing, their laughter evaporating into nothingness, followed closely by harrowing screams. I can hear them all pleading with their mothers to save them; cries of terror and despair. Then the children ignite as they try to run, trails of smoke ghosting behind their bodies and I experience an overwhelming wave of sadness.

The blue sky is now invisible to my eyes. I'm sure it is still there, but all I can see is a grey cloud and whatever was emitted into the air. It's hard to breathe. I can feel my lungs sticking together. Everything is now drenched in red and yellow hues and like a waterfall in reverse, the grey cloud sucks all light and sound towards it.

It'll all be over soon, I'm sure.

A wave of liquid fire spreads effortlessly across the land, disintegrating everything in its path. The city in the distance collapses before my eyes. Buildings turn to ash before disappearing behind the ever-expanding redness. And what I can't see is the wall of sound, a destabilising force that's cleared a path for the wave to pursue.

When it reached my village, I could no longer feel pain, nor breath. Cars and buses blew off the road, while overhead, objects flew in every direction. And those who were left standing pressed their hands against their ears, begging for it all to stop.

I could no longer hear the birds or the sounds of farming, only rumbling horror. The wave was close now as my skin started to melt, sloughing off my body. Below, everyone in the playground was enduring the same fate. The great crying had stopped and children of ash blew apart as if they never existed.

All that remained was a stone wall, between us, imminent destruction. I could feel my body fall, unsupported bone crumbling against the force of death. My eyes melted from their sockets and the last thing I saw was red, before everything I've ever known plunged into total and permanent darkness.

ACKNOWLEDGEMENTS

A very special acknowledgement goes out to Brian Smyth, Lydia Capuano, Boz Mugabe, Kenneth W. Cain, Marie O'Regan, Sadie Hartmann, Steve Stred, Ray Palen, Ben Eads, Chris Rush, Eamon Ó Cléirigh, Jason Cavallaro, Mike Griffin, Brian J. Showers, Stephen Devlin, Nuzo Onoh, Trevor Kennedy, Gemma Amor, John Langan, Philip Fracassi, Tim Lebbon and Adam Nevill.

Finally, dear reader, thank you for taking a punt on this book. I hope I've kept you entertained and we meet again soon.

ABOUT THE AUTHOR

SEÁN O'CONNOR is an award-nominated author, primarily known for his work in Horror and Dark Fiction. He and his family currently reside in Dublin, Ireland.

WWW.SEANOCONNOR.ORG